For Jen—my first best friend.

D0107254

One

"This is going to be awful," my mom says for the millionth time.

"I wish you'd just go home," I tell her. "I'll be fine by myself."

"We've been through this, Gerri. Sixteen is too young to hang around with a bunch of strangers overnight."

"Mom, there's nobody here but music nerds," I say, turning to glance at the line that's rapidly growing behind us. We've been standing outside the university building for less than an hour, but even though it's early in the evening and auditions don't start until the morning, there must be at least a few hundred people here already.

"You're young," she says. "You don't realize how much danger lurks around every corner."

"Give me a break," I say. I can tell from looking around the crowd that I'm not the only one with parental supervision, but that doesn't make it any less annoying.

"I need to take a walk," she says. "I'm going to get a coffee. You want anything?"

"A toasted coconut donut and a green tea." I've heard that green tea is what Adele drinks before every performance. That and whiskey, which I'm obviously not old enough to drink.

Mom kisses me on the forehead and begins cutting through the snaking line, finally emerging on the other side of the crowd and giving me a quick wave before crossing to the coffee shop on the other side of the street.

"Your mom's a little stressed out, hey?" the girl in front of me says out of the blue.

"You could say that." I laugh. "She just hates the whole idea of me getting judged for something like singing."

"But let me guess," she says. "There was no way you were going to let her keep you from auditioning. Am I right?"

"Totally," I say. "I only turned sixteen a few months ago, so this is my first chance to try out. *Big Time*'s my favorite show ever."

"So what do you think so far?" she asks.

"What do I think about what?"

"You know"—she gestures at the people all around us—"all this. The freak show."

"I think it's pretty cool."

As if on cue, a group of dudes nearby start harmonizing "Sweet Caroline" in vibrating falsettos.

"Cool, eh?" she asks, raising an eyebrow. We both laugh.

"Well, maybe not cool, but definitely interesting."

"I'll give you that." She holds out her hand. "I'm Poppy."

"Gerri," I tell her, reaching out to shake.

Poppy looks to be a few years older than me—probably close to the cutoff age, which is twenty-two. She's got beautiful glossy ringlets, and her skin is equally gorgeous, luminous and smooth, the color of the oak desk in my father's office. She's wearing green eye shadow and an ankle-length off-white dress with bright flowers embroidered all over it. I start to worry that maybe I'm underdressed. I'm in my favorite blue sundress with my hair pulled back into a simple ponytail. I look okay, but not nearly as put together as Poppy.

"I love your dress," I tell her.

"Thanks," she says. "Maybe it's overkill, but I want to look good for the judges."

"What kind of stuff do you sing?"

"Oh, this and that. Motown, soul, a little jazz, some Janis Joplin, a bit of opera."

"This and that is right!" I laugh. "Opera?"

"The opera's mainly with my vocal teacher," she says. "I've been taking lessons since I was a little kid. Mostly I sing in church with my mom and my aunt. What about you?"

I'm a little embarrassed to talk about it, although I know I'm going to have to suck it up if I truly want to perform in front of people.

"I've never taken lessons or anything like that," I admit. "My granddad's a really good guitar player, and I guess I kind of started singing along with him, but that's about it. I mostly sing country music. Not a lot of new country. Older stuff."

I can feel my face turning red. A lot of people don't like country music. Definitely not people like Poppy, who obviously has cooler taste than me. To my surprise, though, she's nodding.

"Patsy Cline and Marla Belle Munro? Stuff like that?"

"Yeah," I say. "Marla Belle's my favorite. You like that stuff?"

"Oh yeah," she says, surprising me. "I've got mad respect for the old-timers. They knew how to sing a song for real. No computers backing you up, just a microphone and a big old recording machine."

"That's what my granddad always says," I tell her. "They call the oldies goodies for a reason."

"What's your last name?" she asks. "You need a good last name to sing country music."

"Jones," I tell her.

"Gerri Jones." She grins. "That'll work just fine."

Mom arrives in a big flurry, shoving her way through the lineup and handing me a donut and a cup of tea.

"Thanks. Mom, this is Poppy."

They shake. "I don't think I'll ever understand the appeal of this," says Mom. "Standing in a lineup for twelve hours. Sleeping on concrete."

"Mom!" I say. "I told you a million times, just go home. I'll be fine!"

"You wish," says Mom.

"If you want to go home," says Poppy to my mom, "I don't mind keeping an eye on her. We can watch out for each other."

I turn to look at her, surprised. She looks like she means it.

Mom lifts an eyebrow. "No, I should probably stick around." I can tell she's tempted though.

"I really don't mind," says Poppy. "I'm twenty. Safe and responsible. Took care of my little sister all through school."

Mom makes a big show of thinking it over, although I can tell she's already made up her mind. She's been complaining about having to sleep outside ever since she agreed to come to the audition with me.

"Well," she says finally, "if you're sure."

"I'm totally sure," says Poppy. I shoot her a quick smile.

"Okay, well then, I think I'll go home and have a nice warm bath, watch some TV and get myself ready for bed," says Mom. "Sure you don't want to come with me?"

"Mom! Come on!"

"Okay, fine." She pulls some money out of her purse. "Don't let yourself get hungry, and make sure you buy Poppy something to eat too. You'll text and keep me on top of things?"

"Yes, Mom, I'll text you," I say, wishing she'd hurry up and leave. She got an iPhone for Christmas and is very proud of her texting abilities.

"Thanks a million," I say to Poppy after Mom has left.

She laughs. "No problem at all. I think she would have made you all kinds of nervous if she'd stuck around."

"No kidding."

It starts to get cold as soon as the sun goes behind the building, and by the time it's dark out, I'm really happy that I brought my sleeping bag. I unzip it and pull it tightly around me like a blanket. Now that the reality has sunk in that we're here for the long haul, people are starting to talk to one another. A group of sisters behind us are really funny. They admit outright that they aren't good singers—they just hope to get on TV. I notice a really cute guy sitting by himself a few people in front of Poppy. He has dark curly hair pushed down under a ballcap, and he's holding a guitar that he strums constantly, although you can barely hear it.

The atmosphere is fun and energized, and at some point people start singing. It doesn't take long for the music to move around, like the wave at a hockey game. The harmonies sound great. When one song finishes, another one starts up somewhere else. I'm too shy to sing really loud, although people on all sides of me are starting to get into it, so I sing quietly along to the lyrics I know.

Poppy smiles at me. "You've got a really nice voice," she says. "I bet you'll do great tomorrow." She's just been humming along to the music, not singing at all, so I don't really know what she sounds like. Then, at a lull in the music, she surprises me when she opens her mouth as if it's no big thing and starts to sing.

Ooo-ooh I bet you wonder how I knew
'Bout your plans to make me blue...

She has an incredible voice, big and rich and resonant. I see people in the crowd watching her, as impressed as I am. By the time she makes it to the chorus, it seems as if everyone's singing along.

Eventually, things get a little bit quieter and people begin to settle in for the night. I text my mom to say that things are going well and I'm going to sleep, then curl up and try to make myself comfortable. The last thing I hear before I doze off is the soft, gentle sound of the cute guy's guitar, serenading me to sleep.

Two

I wake up to Poppy nudging me.

"Line's moving," she says. "Time to get a move on."

I yawn and sit up. All around me, bleary-looking people are stretching, rubbing the sleep out of their eyes. I hope I perk up soon, because it seems unlikely that I'll pull off much of an audition in this condition.

Once the doors are opened, the process is surprisingly quick. At the top of the steps, we're handed pins with numbers on them and herded into the giant entry hall.

Inside the building, there's no time to sit and sing. A man with a bullhorn tells us to look at the maps of the building that are taped to the walls around the room.

"Find the floor and room number that corresponds to your pin and go to that room. I suggest you move quickly. We'll be starting auditions soon, and if you aren't in your assigned room when we start to call numbers, you're out of luck."

My pin reads *5* and Poppy's *18*. The map tells us we're in totally different parts of the building. She takes my hand and gives it a squeeze.

"Go get 'em, Gerri Jones," she says with a wink. She heads into the crowd, and I take a deep breath and head off to find my room.

Room 5 is a classroom on the main floor, looking out toward a parking lot. I get there and grab a seat at a desk, watching as people fill up the space—about thirty of us by the time people stop trickling in. I'm happy to see that cute guitar guy is also in this group. He sits on the other side of the room, carefully leaning his guitar against the wall beside him.

The room is full of nervous energy and, unlike last night, nobody seems to feel like singing.

The girl in front of me turns around. "Do you think they're going to audition us in here?"

"I doubt it," I say. "They must have a room set up somewhere with cameras and lights and stuff."

"Yeah," she says. "You're right. They'll probably take us out of here one at a time."

After about half an hour, a young blond woman with a clipboard and a headset hustles into the room. She drops a stack of paper and a bag full of pencils on a table at the side of the classroom and claps her hands for our attention.

"Okay," she says, "you guys are up in fifteen minutes. Here's how it's going to work. You each get to sing just a couple of lines from one song, so make it count. There will be no redos. Any questions?"

The girl in front of me puts up her hand. "Is Maria here? Or Tim and GG? Are they going to hear us?"

Maria, Tim and GG are the *Big Time* judges. Maria Tillerman is a Canadian pop star from the nineties who is always nice to contestants, even when she's telling them they suck. Tim Canon is the mean judge. He looks kind of like Count Chocula and frequently makes people cry. GG, short for Gurmant Gupta, is the quiet judge. He sits back and only gives criticism when he has something to say.

"No," says the clipboard lady. "This is the first round. You'll be singing right here in this room for someone from the production staff. If you make it through this round, you'll have a chance to come back tomorrow to sing for the judges."

A buzz runs through the room at the news.

"How come we don't see that on TV?" asks a guy at the front of the room.

"Because that would be boring," she responds. "The judges don't have time to listen to a thousand people in a day, so we narrow the field for them." She looks at her watch. "You guys have ten minutes. I suggest that you use the time to figure out what you're going to sing. Remember, just a couple of lines. We need to keep things moving." She taps on the pile of paper at the front of the room. "Feel free to write down the words. If you make it through to the judges, you won't have the lyrics in front of you."

She leaves the room and closes the door behind her. Immediately, the room explodes with nervous chatter.

"What's going on?" asks one girl. "This isn't what I expected!"

"It makes sense, doesn't it?" someone responds. "The judges don't have time to see all of us individually. Besides, there's not much we can do about it, right?"

I stare at my paper for a while, thinking through the songs I've been practicing for weeks, trying to figure out which one has the best opening. A couple of lines isn't much material to make a good first impression. By the time the door to the room opens again, it's obvious from the sounds of scribbling and scratching that a lot of people are pretty stressed out, myself included. It feels like we're writing a pop quiz.

Clipboard lady comes back into the room, followed by a tall gray-haired man in jeans and a rumpled, untucked dress shirt. He drags a desk to the front of the room and perches on the edge of it, facing us.

"So," he says, smiling. "Are you guys nervous enough yet?"

He seems genuinely pleasant, and people laugh a little bit, but nobody says anything.

"My name is Bill and I'm the production manager on season nine of *Big Time*." He gestures toward clipboard lady. "I know that Kelly here has given you guys a rundown, so let's get started. I'm going to randomly point at people. When I point at you, stand up, give me your name, your age and the song you'll be singing from, and then go for it. Remember, you only have one chance to impress me, so do your best. Don't be nervous, just relax and have fun!"

Easy for him to say, I think.

He points at a tall girl with braids. She stands up slowly, obviously unhappy to be going first, and tells him that her name is Martha, she's seventeen, and she'll be singing from "Falling," by Alicia Keys.

Smart, I think. *If she can pull it off, she can drag those first lines out and really make an impression.* That style of singing, with runs and acrobatics, isn't up my alley, but I kind of wish it was.

It turns out that Martha can't pull it off, and Bill politely thanks her and points her to the door. She grabs her bag and hustles out of the room. She is soon followed by another girl, who attempts to sing something from the Beatles and forgets the words, although they're right in front of her. Next up is a boy who does what I think is a pretty decent job of a One Direction song.

Bill doesn't agree, apparently, and the boy grabs his bag and follows the other two out the door.

The next singer is a weird-looking girl with a husky voice. She's wearing a straw hat, a tutu and a T-shirt with a picture of a kitten in a wagon on it. She informs us cheerfully that she's nineteen and her name is Babette Gaudet, and then she proceeds to totally butcher "Any Man of Mine," by Shania Twain. She's shrill and loud and totally off-key, and I have to resist the impulse to cover my ears, but to my surprise, Bill claps and tells her to stay.

Cute boy is called upon, and I learn that his name is Keith, he's seventeen, and he's even cuter when he's singing. He has a nice deep voice and does a great job of a Jack Johnson song. I look across the room and smile at him when he's asked to stick around, but I'm not sure if he notices me or not.

By the time we're about halfway through the auditions—a process that has taken less than half an hour—more than twice as many people have been asked to leave as have been told to stay. Suddenly, the girl ahead of me turns around to look at me, and I realize that I'm up.

I slowly stand and force myself to smile, hoping I don't look as nervous as I feel.

"Hi, I'm Gerri," I say. "I'm sixteen, and I'll be singing 'The Best Us We Can Be,' by Marla Belle Munro."

Bill nods and I take a deep breath. I can feel all the eyes in the room on me, but I try not to notice.

I've been thinking a lot about you,
I've been paying attention to me...

I've sung this song a million times with my granddad, and the lyrics come naturally.

I've been spending lots of time daydreamin'
about how we can be the best us we can be...

My impulse is to keep going, but I realize my chance has come and gone in what couldn't have been more than five seconds, and I stop singing, my mouth still hanging open as if it's confused and wondering why my brain has stopped the show so quickly.

The few moments seem to last forever, and then I realize Bill is smiling and nodding at me.

"Nice job, Gerri. Please take a seat and stick around."

I'm moving on to the judges' round, and I can hardly believe it. My head is swimming, and I feel my heart take a luxurious dip into my stomach before lifting back up into my chest and starting to slow back down to normal.

"Nice work!" whispers the girl in front of me, and I smile at her. I glance across the room at cute Keith and realize that he's grinning straight at me, a thumb held up in congratulations.

Three

On the big day, my mom goes through my closet with me to help me figure out what I should wear. I don't want to wear something boring again, so we pick out an embroidered blouse, a short (but not too short) denim skirt and my favorite calf-length brown leather boots. I'm not sure what to do with my hair until Mom suggests I pull it back with a simple red band. I don't look flashy, but I look pretty good, if I do say so myself.

Dad follows us out to the car as we're leaving and gives me a big hug.

"Go get 'em, tiger!" he says.

"Keep your fingers crossed," I tell him.

"You don't need luck, sweetheart. Just be yourself and you can't help but charm them."

The final auditions are in a fancy hotel down-town. Once in the lobby, we follow the signs into a large ballroom, and I'm happy to see that Poppy is there, although I had no doubt she'd make it through. She spots me from across the room and waves excitedly, then moves through the crowd toward us, dragging a tall handsome guy by the hand.

She gives me a big hug. "I'm so excited that you made it!" she says. "This is Jericho, my boyfriend."

Jericho shakes my hand, then my mom's. "I guess we're here for moral support, hey?" he says to my mom.

"I don't know," says Mom. "I kind of feel like she needs to support me. My nerves are shot!"

Poppy looks as good as she did when I met her, maybe even better. She's wearing a long tapestry skirt and a flowing olive-green top, and she has several chains and amber necklaces draped loosely around her neck.

"So what do we have to do?" I ask her.

"You need to sign up at that table over there," she says, pointing.

A production assistant finds my name on a list. "Gerri Jones," she says. "You're in the first group. Come on with me."

Mom and I follow her out of the ballroom and onto an elevator, then down a couple of long hallways. Outside some double doors we find a bunch of chairs, full of contestants and their friends and families. I recognize Babette Gaudet right away. Her hair is in two giant braids and she has on a full cowboy outfit, complete with fringed vest, sequined boots and an enormous cowboy hat.

"Mercy," my mom mutters. "That girl took the wrong turn on the way to the rodeo."

"You guys have a seat here," the production assistant tells us. "They're going to start calling people in soon. You're one of ten contestants in this first batch." She points out some duct tape that makes a half circle in front of the doors. "When you stand inside this line, you're on camera. They want to be able to catch the reactions of everyone as they come out of the room. You have your song ready?"

I nod.

"Great. Try to relax. It's pretty easy when you get in there. There's a pathway marked in tape, and a large rectangle on the floor with the *Big Time* logo on it. Just walk right up and stand directly on it. They'll tell you what to do from there."

"Okay," I say.

"Good luck," she says and walks away.

Mom and I grab seats. Nobody is speaking—everyone's too nervous. After what seems like an eternity, the door opens and a young man sticks his head out.

"Frank Polito?" he asks.

A tall guy sitting a few seats over gets up, gives the guy he's with a high five and saunters into the audition room.

Everyone in the waiting area is on high alert for the next few minutes, leaning forward in their seats and trying to hear what's going on. It's useless though—the hotel walls are just too thick.

Finally, Frank comes out of the room. He looks really sad at first, but then he jumps in the air and hoots. "I made it!" he yells. His friend runs over and they hug and jump up and down.

"I'm not doing that if you make it," my mom whispers.

Next up is Babette Gaudet. She cheerfully flounces into the room, and she's in there for a long time.

"I can't for the life of me imagine what she's singing," says Mom.

Finally, the door swings open and Babette stomps out, ripping her cowboy hat off.

"If you just wanted someone to make fun of," she yells back into the room, "you could have let me know and saved us all a lot of trouble!"

One of the show workers hurries up and ushers her out of the waiting area.

I don't have much time to register all of this, because a production assistant sticks his head out of the audition room and calls my name. Mom squeezes my knee and I stand up, trying not to show my nerves as I walk through the door the PA is holding open for me.

It's a relatively small room, but there are a lot of people and even more equipment crammed into it. I glance around quickly and see that there are several cameras, a bunch of lights on stands and cables everywhere. At the back of the room is a table, set up in front of a large window with a view of the harbor. The judges are sitting there, expressionless, as I come into the room.

I walk between the taped-off lines and stand on the *Big Time* logo like I was told.

"What's your name?" asks Tim Canon abruptly.

"Um, Gerri Jones?"

"Are you asking me or telling me, Um Gerri Jones?"

I try to smile, but I'm already feeling bad about this.

"My name is Gerri Jones," I say, trying to sound cheerful and calm although I'm neither.

"That wasn't so hard, was it?" he says. I don't know what to say, he's being so rude to me.

Thankfully, GG decides to speak up.

"What are you going to sing for us today, Gerri?" he asks.

"I'm going to sing 'Gimme One Good Reason to Stay,' by Marla Belle Munro," I tell him.

"Great song," murmurs Maria Tillerman.

"Okay," says Tim. "Take it away."

My heart is pounding, but I take a deep breath, smile, close my eyes and start to sing.

You haven't smiled at me in weeks,
You don't have one nice thing to say,
I lie awake every night waiting for you to
    come home,
So gimme one good reason to stay...

This song is one of my granddad's favorites—one of my favorites too—and after a couple of moments I start to get into the music. I've made it to the end of the first verse and taken a deep breath to get me through the chorus when Tim Canon throws his hand up.

"Stop!" he says. So I do.

I stand looking at them, wondering what's going on.

"I'm sorry," he says. "The problem isn't your voice. Your voice is fine. The problem is that you're just too boring. You actually might be one of the most boring performers I've ever encountered in twenty-five years in show business."

I stand there, my mouth going dry. I don't know what to say.

"Okay," I manage to squeak out.

"I'm a no-go," he says. "No way, no how."

He turns to GG, who just shakes his head slowly.

Maria turns and glares pointedly at Tim, then leans forward in her seat, rests her chin in one hand and smiles at me. "Honey," she says, "you have a real good voice, you really do. Don't listen to this jackass over here. I think the—"

"Maria," interrupts one of the clipboard people from the edge of the set. "You can't say that. Back up."

Maria sits back in her seat, pauses for a few moments. Then she leans forward and starts again, saying everything exactly the same way for the cameras.

"Honey," she says, "you have a real good voice, you really do. Don't listen to this—to Tim over here. I think the problem is that you aren't quite the right fit for the show. You need to get out there and get some experience on a stage, then maybe come back again next year and give it another shot."

I've seen this happen on *Big Time* before. Some shy, nervous person has a good voice, but they don't have stage presence. I've seen some of them protest, claim that they can learn, that they can shake off their nerves and do a better job down the road. Sometimes they even manage to convince the judges, who decide to toss out a second chance, to bring them all the way to the show so that they can have another opportunity to prove themselves.

I wish I had the guts to say something like that, but I don't. All I want is to get out of the room. My mouth opens and I hear myself croak out "Okay" for the second time.

Then I'm being ushered out the door and into the waiting area.

Everyone in the room is watching the door when it opens and I'm shuffled out by a production assistant. The door shuts behind him with a soft *ka-thunk*, and it's all over. I look around, confused, until I spot my mom, who's getting up from her chair slowly, expectantly. I just shake my head and realize there's a good chance I'm going to start crying.

"Oh, sweetie," says Mom as she comes up and gives me a hug.

"Where do we go?" I ask, pulling away from her, my voice coming out a lot louder than I expect. I try not to meet the eyes of any of the other people in the waiting area.

Another production assistant comes over and smiles at me. He puts his hand on my back and guides me through a doorway and into an empty hallway. My mom hurries along beside me.

"I don't know if they were mean to you or not," the PA says. "If they were, try not to take it personally. They just do it for TV."

"Well, that's reassuring," snaps Mom.

He smiles sympathetically and heads back to the waiting area.

Mom moves around to face me.

"You okay?"

I nod, but I can feel the tears starting to come.

"Oh, sweetie," she says again. "What can I do?"

"I need to find a bathroom," I blubber. "I'll be okay, I just need to find a bathroom."

We walk down the hallway until we find a ladies' room. "You want me to come in?" she asks.

I shake my head. "Just give me a few minutes."

Thankfully, it's empty. I lean into the sink and cry a little bit, just for a couple of minutes. I manage to compose myself, then wash my face. It feels good. I stare into the mirror. My eyes are a bit pink, but I look okay.

There's nothing I can do about it now. As I turn to leave, the door to the washroom opens and Maria Tillerman pushes through. She stops when she sees me.

"Oh," she says.

"I was just leaving," I say and start to move past her.

"Hang on, honey," she says. I stop and look at her, trying my best to smile.

"What's your name again?" she asks. "I know it was just a few minutes ago, but I see so many people."

"Gerri Jones," I tell her.

"That's right. Listen, Gerri," she says, "this is the way the show works. You shouldn't take it to heart. I can guarantee you they won't use your clips on TV—you were too good for that."

"That doesn't make any sense," I tell her.

"Look at it this way. There are people who are born to get onstage and belt out songs, and they have loads of charisma and stage presence. Those are the people we take for the show. Then there are the people who are terrible, who we let through the process because they come across as funny, like that cowgirl who came in before you. It might not be the nicest thing in the world, but we need people who'll make good TV.

"Then there are the people with good voices who haven't quite figured out the stage presence thing. People like you. The good news is that you can learn the stage-presence stuff, but you can never teach someone how to have a good voice. You have a really good voice. I hope you remember that. Music should be fun, not stressful. I hope you keep singing, because you've got an instrument, girl. It would be a shame for you to waste it."

"Thanks," I say.

"I mean it. Now I had better do my business and get out of here before they send in the troops after me."

She goes into a stall and locks the door.

The last thing I hear as I leave is a muffled "Good luck, Gerri Jones."

Four

On the drive home, Mom rants and raves about the whole *Big Time* process.

"What is wrong with those people?" she says as we peel out of the parking lot. "I mean, look at you, you're adorable! You've got the voice of a honky-tonk angel! They're crazy!"

"What's a honky-tonk angel?" I ask.

"It doesn't matter," she says. "I'm trying to tell you that the system is obviously rigged, Gerri. The fix is in. The jig is up."

"You make it sound like a big conspiracy," I say. "They just didn't like me."

"Don't ignore the facts," she says. "If it looks like a duck and talks like a duck, you're probably dealing with a duck. Let's pick up some pizza for supper. There's no way I'm cooking tonight."

Dad is waiting by the front door when we get home, smiling and expectant. His smile fades when he sees me.

"No?" he asks.

I just shake my head.

"Oh, sweetie," he says. "It's their loss, that's for sure."

"They made her cry," my mother says.

"They didn't make me cry," I say. "I was just emotional because I got my hopes up. It was stupid of me to think I'd make it."

"They did too make you cry," she says. "Grown adults insulting impressionable teenagers to their faces. It isn't right."

"It most certainly wasn't stupid of you to think you'd make it," says my father. "You have a fantastic voice. What on earth did they find to criticize, exactly?"

I glance behind me and catch my mother making a throat-slitting gesture.

"Never mind," he says.

"They said I was boring and had no stage presence," I say.

"That's crazy!" he says. "These people are obviously amateurs who wouldn't know talent if it punched them in the face."

"Kind of the opposite," I say. "They're professionals who do this for a living."

"Just hang on a second, okay?" He runs into the living room and comes back with one hand behind his back.

"Ta da!" he says, holding out a bouquet of Gerbera daisies, my favorite flower.

"Your father and I bought you some flowers just because you're our favorite daughter," says Mom. "Nothing to do with *Big Time*, just a random gift."

"It says *Congratulations*," I say, peering down at the little card nestled inside the flowers.

"Congratulations on being our favorite daughter," says Dad. "And on having the guts to audition."

"Thanks."

"I'll put them in some water," says Mom. "Why don't you go up and tell your brother to come down for supper?"

My brother, Jack, is in his room studying, with his back to the door and his giant headphones on.

I can never understand how he's able to concentrate on schoolwork while listening to his insane punk music, but his marks sure don't suffer. He's pretty much a genius who will end up curing some disease or inventing a new social network. He has his music jacked up so loud that I have to smack my hand on his wall several times before he realizes I'm standing in the doorway.

"How'd it go?" he asks, swiveling around in his chair.

"Not good."

"Sucks," he says. "You're better off anyway. Have you ever seen how stupid they make people on that show look?"

"I guess so," I say. "It's still no fun though. Mom wants you to come down for supper. We picked up pizza."

The whole time we eat, my parents won't stop talking about the *Big Time* auditions.

"The thing is, Gerri," my father starts, "you need to remember that music takes a lot of hard work and practice."

"That's why they call it show business," says Mom, "and not show laziness."

"That's a great play on words, Mom," Jack says, his mouth full of pizza.

"Really though," says Dad, "haven't you seen this Justin Boober—"

"Bieber," says Jack.

"Whatever," says Dad. "Bieber. Haven't you seen his documentary? That kid was playing and practicing and practicing and playing and performing—"

"I get the picture, Dad," I say.

"What we're trying to say," says Mom, "is—"

"I know what you're trying to say," I tell them. "Practice makes perfect. Get back on the horse and ride. If I want to take music seriously, I have to start getting serious."

They look surprised.

"Exactly," they say at the same time.

"That's all great advice," I tell them. "I'm just not sure I really want to sing anymore, is all."

"What are you talking about?" asks Mom. "Of course you do! You've been singing since you could barely walk, and you talked about this *Big Time* audition for months."

"Yeah, and look how that turned out," I say. "No offense, guys, but I don't really want to talk about this anymore. Is it okay if I go hang out in my room? I just want to be alone for a while."

"Of course you can, sweetie," says Dad.

"Take the flowers with you," says Mom. "They'll help cheer you up."

I grab the vase and bring it upstairs to my room, placing it on my dresser and stopping for a minute to stare at the old album covers I have stuck on my wall. Loretta Lynn, Patsy Cline and Marla Belle Munro stare out at me, all big hair and bright eyes and wide smiles, hanging on to microphones like their lives depend on it. I wonder if anyone ever told them they were boring, that they lacked stage presence. Somehow I doubt it.

I grab my laptop from my desk and flop onto my bed. I notice right away that I have a friend request and a new message. It's from Poppy.

Hey you! Hopefully this is Gerri Jones from the Big Time auditions, otherwise ignore this message because I'll sound like a crazy person! How did your audition go? I asked a production assistant in the waiting area, but she told me they couldn't give me any info about other contestants. Guess what? I made it! I'm flying to Toronto in a week for sudden-death round. Eek! Anyway, holla at me when you have a minute. Kisses! Poppy.

I'm not surprised that Poppy made it. Not only does she have a killer voice, but she's got me beat hands down when it comes to stage presence. I'm sure she was able to waltz into the audition room and shine that big smile at the judges and convince them that she's got what it takes for *Big Time*, maybe even to go all the way. I'm not jealous, exactly. I'm really happy for Poppy, but I can't help wishing I had her star quality. I guess some of us are born for the stage and some of us aren't.

I send her back a quick note, congratulating her and telling her my own news. She replies almost instantly.

They don't know what they're missing, Gerri. You'll just have to come back next year and show them how wrong they were. Wish me luck and promise you'll meet me for coffee when I get back to town. It'll probably be sooner than later haha! Xoxo. P.

I'm supposed to call my friend Meg and fill her in on how the audition went, but I don't feel like going over everything yet again. Instead I just lie on my bed, staring at the ceiling. I know my parents are right, that real musicians work really hard to be good at what they do. The thing is, I've been watching *Big Time* religiously since I was seven years old, and I know enough to realize that when someone comes in with enough raw talent, the judges will snatch them up and teach them *how* to work hard and get where they need to go. I've been waiting patiently for the day I became old enough to audition, preparing for the moment when I'd finally get to prove myself, and now that moment has come and gone. I've missed my big opportunity.

Now Poppy's about to be whisked away to Toronto, to the stage I've imagined walking onto for years, and I'm at home in my room. It was nice of Maria Tillerman to give me some words of encouragement, but I know I'll never try out for *Big Time* again. I'd have to be able to show up next year and convince them that I'm a totally different person. It doesn't matter how much practicing I do between now and then, I'm never going to be what they want me to be.

Five

Meg comes running up to my locker the next morning before I've even had a chance to hang up my jacket.

"Okay, what the heck?" she says. "What happened? Why didn't you call me?"

"Sorry, I didn't feel like talking about it."

"Oh no!" she says. "The jerks didn't take you?"

I just shake my head as I pull out my math book and shut my locker.

"Ugh," she says, hurrying to keep up as I walk down the hallway to Mr. Romo's room. "So what happened, anyway?"

"I still don't feel like talking about it," I tell her.

"Oh come on, Gerri!" she says. "You're the closest thing I have to a celebrity friend! How else am I going to live vicariously?"

I laugh. "Celebrity friend? I was rejected from a reality singing show."

"Yeah," she says. "But you got to talk to the judges! And there were cameras pointed at you, right?"

"Seriously, Meg, I just don't want to get into the messy details right now."

"Okay, fine," she says. "Take some time to lick your wounds, but I want to hear all about it by the weekend."

I might not want to talk about it, but that doesn't stop people from asking me about it. Everyone seems to know about the audition, and I have to just grin and bear it as one person after another comes up to find out how things went. I'm grateful when Denny Moir accidentally spills chocolate milk all over Valerie LaMarsh at lunchtime and I become old news.

I'm on my way to the last class of the day when Ms. Kogawa, the music teacher, stops me in the hallway.

"Gerri, I've been looking for you."

I'm surprised, since I don't have music this semester.

"I wonder if you can come see me in the music room after school," she says. "It'll only take a minute."

"Um, I guess so?" I wonder if I'm in trouble about something.

"Don't look so nervous," she says, laughing. "It's not a big deal, but I don't really have time to explain right now."

"Okay," I say. "I'll be there."

I find it hard to concentrate in English class, and I'm happy that I'm not called on to answer any questions about *Lord of the Flies*. As the teacher talks about how the powerful, mean kids make life on the island miserable for the powerless kids, I'm reminded of the *Big Time* judging panel. After school, Meg asks if I want to go to the mall with her, but I tell her I have to stick around. I wait by my locker until everyone's cleared out. Then I walk down to the music room.

Ms. Kogawa looks up from her desk when I come into the room.

"Thanks for coming, Gerri," she says. "Grab a seat."

I pull a chair over and sit across from her desk.

"I'll get right to the point," she says. "I heard through the grapevine that you tried out for that singing show."

Poppy's version of "I Heard It Through the Grapevine" immediately runs through my head, and I smile.

"Yeah," I say. "*Big Time*. I didn't make it."

"I heard that too," she says. "I have to say, I was a bit surprised. You've never joined school band or performed in any of our yearly concerts. I didn't know you were a musician."

"I'm not," I say. "Not really. I just sing a little bit, for fun. I'm not very good."

"What makes you say that?" she asks. "You thought you were good enough to try out for the show, right?"

"Yeah, and then they didn't take me."

She waves her hand as if swatting a fly away. "I wouldn't read too much into that, Gerri. Anyway, enough beating around the bush. I'm starting a choral club, and I wonder if you'd like to join?"

"A choral club?" I ask. "Like on *Glee*?"

"I guess you could say that," she says. "Not nearly as elaborate though. It'll be more of a bare-bones operation, no costumes or chore-ography or pyrotechnics, but it will be a lot of fun. It's extracurricular, but you'll learn a lot too."

I've never considered joining a group chorus. When I've sung in the past, it's always been by myself or with my granddad.

"I don't think it's my thing," I say. "I'm not really into that kind of music."

"What kind of music?" she asks.

"You know, like choir music and stuff."

She laughs. "Well, I don't know if it will change your mind or not, but part of the fun of being in a choral club is picking the songs to sing and coming up with cool arrangements. We can do pretty much any kind of music we're inter-ested in. Everyone will have a say and the group will decide."

"Thanks, Ms. Kogawa, but I don't think it's for me. I appreciate you thinking of me though. Really."

We both stand up and she walks me to the door.

"Well, it never hurts to ask," she says. "If you change your mind, feel free to show up here for our first rehearsal. Sunday at one o'clock."

When I leave the school, I text Meg and then walk to the mall to meet up with her. She's hanging out in the food court, sipping on an Orange Julius and staring blatantly at a group of guys goofing around a couple of tables away from her.

"You're so obvious," I say.

"What are you talking about?" she asks. "Those boys should count themselves lucky that I think they're worth checking out."

I look over at them in time to see one guy stick a French fry up his nose as his buddies laugh like a bunch of orangutans.

"They sure look like a bunch of winners," I say.

"They can't all be Prince Harry," she says. "Come on, I want you to tell me what you think about some shoes I saw at Sexy Pixie."

Usually, helping Meg pick out clothes is the most boring job on earth, but today I'm happy to be distracted, so I follow her up the escalator to the top floor of the mall.

"So what did you need to stick around school for?" she asks.

"Ms. Kogawa wants me to try out for her choral club," I say.

"Whoa," says Meg. "Lame. You told her no, right?"

"Yeah," I say.

"Good," she says. "The last thing your street cred needs is to be seen singing 'Wind Beneath My Wings' with Bernice Sneed and whatever other music geeks Kogawa's rounded up." She shudders. "You'd probably have to do jazz hands and everything."

"I don't think it's like that," I say, but she isn't listening.

"Check out that top!" she says, beelining to the Sexy Pixie store. I'm about to follow her when I catch the eye of a guy coming out of the music store. We recognize each other at the same time. It's Keith, the cute guitar guy from the auditions.

He smiles and walks over to me. "Gerri, right?" he asks.

I can't believe he remembers my name. "Yeah," I say. "Keith?"

"That's right. How's it going? How was your audition yesterday?"

"Ugh," I say. "Not good. They tore me apart."

"I'm sorry to hear that," he says. "But you know what they say, misery loves company. I didn't make it either."

"Wow," I say. "That really surprises me."

"Ditto," he says. "So was Tim Canon really mean to you?"

"Yes!" I say. "He told me I was the most boring performer he'd ever seen!"

"That's nothing," says Keith. "He told me I was an unkempt folksinger wannabe and a simpering cliché."

"What does that even mean?" I ask.

"I have no idea," he says. "But I'm totally gonna write a song called 'Simpering Cliché'." He laughs.

"You write your own songs?"

"Yeah," he says. "Some of them. I do covers and stuff too, but I love writing. I'm kind of happy that I didn't make it onto *Big Time*, because they don't let you do originals. I won't lie though—it was a blow to the ego."

"Tell me about it," I say.

"Oh well, maybe I am a cliché. But I'm not going to give up playing music because those jerks didn't like me."

I just nod, thinking that it must be nice to have real musical talent. Keith's the real deal, not a poser like me.

"I should get going," he says. "I'm supposed to meet my dad in the parking lot. Cool seeing you, Gerri."

"Yeah, you too," I say.

I watch as he disappears into the crowd. I'm not even aware that Meg has walked up next to me until she reaches out and pokes me.

"You're so obvious," she says.

"Cut it out," I say, blushing.

"Who was that shaggy masterpiece?" she asks.

"Just a guy I met at the auditions."

"Maybe it wasn't such a waste of *Big Time* after all," she says. "Did you get his number?"

"No," I say. "It wasn't like that."

She rolls her eyes at me. "Gerri, you need a life coach, do you know that?"

Six

On Saturday I decide to visit my granddad at the seniors' residence where he lives. Lilac Grove Retirement Complex is way out in the suburbs, so I have to make two bus transfers and then walk several blocks to get there. I don't mind, though, because it's a nice day. When I arrive at Lilac Grove, lots of elderly folks are wandering about the grounds, but not Granddad. I know exactly where I'll find him.

Sure enough, he's on the wide back veranda, happily strumming on his guitar and smiling down at the other residents who pass in front of him as they wander through the flower gardens.

"Gerri!" he says, waving happily when he sees me. "How's my girl?"

"I'm great, Granddad," I say, leaning down to hug him. "How are you?"

"Well, it's hard to complain on a day like this," he says. "Have a seat."

I pull a wicker chair up beside his bench and sit down.

"What were you playing?" I ask.

In response, his fingers begin to pick out a cheerful bluegrass melody that I recognize right away. After a few bars, he starts singing.

You are my sunshine, my only sunshine
You make me happy when times are gray...

I love my granddad's voice. It's sweet and simple, with a soft, husky edge. I smile broadly at him and tap my feet with the rhythm, happy to be listening, but after another verse, he stops abruptly.

"Gerri," he says. "What in blazes is wrong?"

"What do you mean, Granddad?"

"I've been playing that song for you since you weren't even up to my knee," he says. "That's the first time you haven't joined in."

"Sorry," I say. "I guess I don't really feel like singing today. I love listening to you though. You should keep playing."

"Not a chance, sweetheart," he says. "You've gotta pay if you want to hear me play, and the only currency I'll accept is your pretty voice."

He carefully lays his guitar down on the bench next to him and leans in to look me in the eye.

"Tell me what's wrong, Gerri."

"It's no big deal," I say. "It's just this stupid TV show."

"Is this the one you were talking about last time you visited? The singing contest?"

"Yeah," I say. "I had my audition last week. They didn't pick me."

"So now you don't want to sing because some TV people didn't want you on their show?"

"Yeah, I guess," I say, shrugging.

"Are these people friends of yours?" he asks.

"No. They're the judges. They travel to cities around the country and look for talent."

"So some complete strangers didn't much care for your singing, and that bothers you enough that you won't even sing with your dear old granddad the way you have been since you were just a wee little thing?"

"It's not like that," I say, although it kind of is like that.

"Do you remember when I moved in here, Gerri?" he asks me. "How unhappy I was?"

I nod.

"I missed your grandma something fierce," he says. "I missed that little house we spent all those years in, and the garden we planted together. I missed my workshop and my reading chair next to the big brick fireplace. Moving in here felt like a death sentence, like I was giving up my independence."

I remember how sad he was all the time, sitting in his room and staring out the window. Before Lilac Grove, I'd always loved visiting my grandfather, but when he had to sell the house and move into his little apartment, it stopped being fun.

"I remember that," I tell him. "You were depressed."

"I got over it though, didn't I?" he asks. "Do you want to know how?"

"Sure," I say.

"Well, Gerri, I was sitting in my room one day, a few months after I moved in, just staring at the television. I don't even remember what I was watching—probably wasn't even paying attention to it. Anyway, a commercial came on and the jingle in the background was an old country-and-western tune I used to play, and I started kind of humming along and tapping my feet. Before I even realized what I was doing, I was up out of my chair, digging around in the closet."

He reaches over and picks up his guitar. "I hadn't so much as looked at this old girl the whole time I'd been living here, but she was in there waiting for me."

He starts to play a cheerful, fast-paced tune that I recognize right away. This time, when he starts to sing, I lean forward in my chair and join him. I'm still not really in the mood to sing, but I don't want to disappoint him a second time.

Hey, hey, good-lookin'
Whaaaatcha got cookin'?

The funny thing is, as our voices weave together and I fall naturally back into the harmonies that Granddad taught me so many years ago, I start to enjoy myself. There's something really nice about singing with someone whose voice fits well with yours. On the surface, you wouldn't necessarily expect my high young voice to match with Granddad's husky old baritone, but when they blend, a whole new sound emerges. It's hard to know where it even comes from.

He brings the song to a close with a tidy little riff and a couple of pats on the guitar, then reaches over and slaps me on the knee.

"That's more like it!" he says. "Wasn't so bad, was it?"

"It was fun," I agree.

"Music sure helped me get out of that funk," he says. "Far as I'm concerned, it's pretty much the best way we've got to express ourselves. Helps us feel better when we're feeling down, and it helps us bring a little bit of happiness into other people's lives when we're feeling good. One thing it should never be is an excuse for people to judge one another. There's plenty of other reasons to do that without dragging music into the mix."

Two old ladies walk up the steps from the garden and come over to us.

"Oh, wonderful," says one of them. "Nelson has his guitar out!"

"Ladies," says Granddad, "this is my granddaughter, Gerri. Gerri, this is Dina and Lucille."

"Nice to meet you, Gerri," says Dina. "Your grandfather talks about you all the time. Says you've got quite a lovely singing voice."

I laugh. "Oh, I don't know about that."

"Come on, Nelson," says Lucille, dragging a couple of chairs over to join us. "Give us a tune."

"What do you think, Gerri?" says Granddad. "Any requests?"

"How about 'Back in Baby's Arms'?" I say after thinking for a few moments.

"I'm pretty sure I can oblige," he says.

He starts to play, and soon all four of us are belting it out. I glance at Lucille and Dina, their heads thrown back and giant smiles stretched across their faces, and I realize that they don't give a hoot about their stage presence. They're singing because they want to be part of the music, nothing more complicated than that.

* * *

After supper I sit down with my parents to watch the special two-hour season premiere of *Big Time.* The first episode of every season is always focused on auditions. They spend a few minutes on each of the ten audition cities; first they show the big crowds lined up to try out, and then some clips from the audition highlights.

Within the first few minutes of the show, a girl gets rejected, even though I think she has a great voice. I feel bad for her, but I can't help feeling a bit comforted too. A little while later the judges let a guy through even though my parents and I agree that he wasn't very good. I remember that *Big Time* is always like this. You can never really tell what the judges are going to say. Tim Canon is consistent though. He's rude to everyone, even the people he likes—not that it makes me feel much better about the things he said to me.

"Look!" yells my mother excitedly, and I realize they've cut to the big lineup outside the building where I auditioned. There are a few quick shots of the crowd, but I'm not in any of them. The crowd shots are followed immediately by the second day of auditions, making it appear as if they happened on the same day, although I know better. My heart starts to pound. I really hope they don't show my audition, because I don't want to end up on TV looking like an idiot. Poppy appears on the screen almost right away. She strides out in front of the judges as confident as anything and cheerfully announces her name.

"Look!" says Mom. "It's your friend! That girl who babysat you!"

"She didn't 'babysit' me," I say.

Tim Canon says something rude about Poppy's outfit, and Poppy sasses him right back, which gets the other judges laughing and even forces a smile out of Tim.

"She's a natural," says Dad.

Then Poppy sings a gorgeous full-throated rendition of "At Last," by Etta James. The judges can't praise her enough, even Tim, and when she leaves the room the cameras stay on them for a few more seconds.

"That girl is the real deal," says GG as Tim and Maria nod. "She could win the whole thing."

Next, they show Babette Gaudet's audition. She comes marching into the judging area and basically proceeds to bomb out. I'm not surprised, since she was pretty bad in the group audition. Tim Canon rips into her as cheerfully as ever, and even GG gets in on the act, telling Babette she should quit singing altogether. What strikes me is that while she's singing, Babette really does seem to be enjoying herself. She's off-key for sure, but she's smiling and her eyes are closed. You can tell she's really lost in the song. After they rip her apart, though, she looks totally defeated, and she storms out of the room as they continue to laugh at her. Only Maria Tillerman, sitting forward with her elbows on the table and her chin in her hands, doesn't seem to be enjoying the spectacular flameout.

It's not out of the ordinary for the *Big Time* judges to be mean to a contestant, but I feel differently about it this time. I know what it's like to stand in front of them, hoping they'll tell you you're great, only to have them stomp on your self-esteem. It isn't as funny when you know how it feels.

It turns out I have nothing to worry about. Just like Maria Tillerman predicted, I don't show up onscreen at all. After Babette's appearance the show cuts to a commercial, and when it comes back they're on to another city. My audition is lost to history.

When the show's over, I go up to my room and send Poppy a quick message.

Wow! You were amazing! I'm so proud of you, and I know you're going to do great. I'll be voting for you every week.

I pause for a minute before writing the second half of my message.

I've been asked to join a choral group. I think I'm going to give it a shot. Maybe next time you're in town, you'll have a chance to see me sing too.

Seven

On Sunday afternoon I tell my parents that I'm going to the library, and then I bike to the school instead. I don't want to tell anyone that I'm trying out for the choral group until I decide for sure that I want to do it.

It's always weird being at school on a weekend. The hallways are empty and the lights are dim, but as I walk toward the music room, I can hear laughter and chattering. I stand outside the doorway for a moment, then take a breath and walk into the room. The chattering stops as everyone turns to look at me, and Ms. Kogawa, who's stapling some papers at her desk, smiles and raises a hand in greeting.

"Gerri," she says. "You decided to check us out. That's great. Come on in."

I grab a seat next to Bernice Sneed. Bernice is in my year at school, and Meg's right about her being a hardcore music nerd. For as long as I can remember, Bernice has spent her summers at music camp and her weekends taking music lessons. I also recognize a plump smiling girl with short curly hair and a really tall kid who I'm pretty sure is in my brother's class, but I don't know either of their names. On the other side of the room a guy and a girl, both with white-blond hair and bright blue eyes, sit with their backs against the wall. I've never seen them before, but they look so much alike, it's obvious they're related.

"Hey, Gerri," says Bernice. "I didn't know you were trying out for choral."

"I wasn't going to," I say. "But I thought about it some more and figured it wouldn't hurt to give it a chance."

"It's going to be fun," she says. "Ms. Kogawa has been trying to get a choral group off the ground for a couple of years, but she couldn't get enough people interested."

Ms. Kogawa finishes her paperwork and comes around to sit on her desk.

"Okay," she says cheerfully, clapping her hands together. "I was hoping we'd have at least five or six people, so this is great. Good stuff. How about we do a round of introductions?"

I learn that the blond kids, Macy and Davis, are twins and also that they're homeschooled. They go to the same church as Ms. Kogawa, who tells us that they'll be honorary students for choral-club purposes.

Tyler, the tall guy, is a senior who's looking for an extracurricular besides track to help him get into his school of choice. The plump girl, Olive, is a year behind me in school and has been singing for years.

"I'm really just waiting to be old enough to try out for *Big Time*," she says. "I figured this would be great experience."

I notice a weird look flicker across Bernice's face, and I start to feel self-conscious. I wonder what she's heard about my failed audition.

"Let's get down to business," says Ms. Kogawa. She grabs a stack of papers from her desk and passes them around. I take a look at the stapled sheets she's handed me, a bunch of sheet music. I start to get nervous. I don't know how to read music. Granddad taught me to play a couple of simple chords on a guitar, but that's about it.

"I'd like to start by getting a feel for who sings in what range," she says. "Who wants to take a crack at piano?" I look around, surprised when Bernice, Olive and Macy all put their hands up to volunteer.

"Great," says Ms. Kogawa. "I'm glad to learn that I don't have a shy group. How about you do the honors today, Bernice? The rest of you, don't worry—everyone will have a chance."

I'm relieved when Tyler puts his hand up and asks the same thing that I've been thinking.

"Are we expected to be able to read music? 'Cause I don't sight-read."

"Who else doesn't read music?" she asks. Only Tyler and I put up our hands, and I begin to wonder what I've gotten myself into. She didn't mention being able to read music when she told me about the choral group.

"That's okay," she says. "You don't necessarily need to be able to do it to start off. It will help if you're willing to put some time into at least learning the basics. We'll always do a careful run-through of the various parts before we really dig into a new piece. If you've got a good ear, it should be no problem, and I'll be happy to give the two of you some extra help to bring you up to speed in the meantime."

Tyler glances over at me, and I can tell by the look on his face that he's as skeptical as I am. I'm not about to stand up and leave in the middle of practice though, so I wait to see what happens.

"The songs I've handed out are just for practice," Ms. Kogawa says. "Once we're off and running, we'll start to develop a set list and come up with some ideas for future performances."

"Where will we be performing?" asks Bernice.

"There's nothing lined up yet," says Ms. Kogawa. "I wanted to make sure I could pull a group together before I started looking for venues."

Our first song is a Broadway show tune. I don't recognize the name, but as soon as Bernice plays the intro, I realize that I've actually heard it a million times, and although I wouldn't know the words to save my life, the tune immediately pops into my head.

I soon discover that choral singing isn't quite as simple as knowing a basic melody. The vocals are broken into four parts—bass, tenor, alto and soprano—and each of them has a separate melody line. Individually, they sound kind of funny, twisting up or down and away from the tune I'm familiar with, but it becomes clear when we sing the components together that the whole sounds better than the sum of its parts. It's like when I harmonize with my granddad, but more formal.

It's obvious when I think about it. I've never had a problem singing harmonies—they've just come naturally to me. Although I have no idea how to read sheet music, I start to think about how instinct can only take you so far. Seeing a simple melody broken apart and written down for multiple voices gives me a whole new perspective on how music works.

As Bernice leads us through the song on the piano, Ms. Kogawa writes our names on the board under the various vocal parts. It turns out that Tyler and Davis both sing tenor, Bernice and Macy are altos, and Olive and I are sopranos. I've always known my voice is in the high register, but it's never occurred to me to think of myself as a soprano. It sounds really professional, although

I sure don't feel that way, especially compared to the rest of them, who've obviously been taking music lessons forever.

To my surprise, things actually start to come together pretty quickly. I've always had an easy time catching on to a tune, and this is really no different. Olive and I run through our part a couple of times, and once everyone else has had the chance to do the same with their parts, we try doing it together. It doesn't sound perfect, and there are a couple of places where I lose the melody and have to stop for a second before I can pick it up again, but it sounds better than I would have expected. It's amazing to think that music can be approached this way, like a puzzle that has a correct solution.

"I think that's great for today, guys," says Ms. Kogawa once we've run through the song a few times. "We'll have to do our best to find a guy or two to sing bass, but other than that, it sounded really good. I'm happy to say that I think everyone is going to fit into the group."

It's been so much fun working out the details of the song, I've completely forgotten that this is actually an audition. I'm surprised to find that

I'm excited to hear I've made the cut—for now, at least. Maybe my parents were right about throwing myself into music and improving through hard work. Maybe it won't be that bad after all, although I can only imagine what Meg will say when she hears.

"You were really good on piano," I say to Bernice as we're putting on our coats. She looks at me as if she's surprised.

"What, you mean today?" she asks. "Thanks, but that's nothing. I've got a background in piano. I've been playing since I was four. This was just plunking out the melody line."

"Gerri and Tyler, do you mind sticking around for a minute?" Ms. Kogawa asks. We hold back as everyone else leaves. When they've cleared out, she comes around to sit on the front of her desk. "You guys did a really good job today. It isn't always easy to keep up when everyone else has some theory and is able to read music. That said, I do think you could both benefit from a bit of extra training. Are you able to come by here for, say, a half hour or so on Tuesdays after school for the next few weeks?"

"Works for me," says Tyler.

"Yeah," I say. "I can do that."

"Good," she says. "It'll be fun to see where we end up over the next little while."

Eight

As I suspected, Meg thinks the whole thing is insane.

"What do you think you're going to gain from singing with a choral club?" she asks.

It's after school on Tuesday, and I've just explained to her that I can't go to the mall with her because I have to get some extra help from Ms. Kogawa.

"I don't know." I shrug. "I just want to learn more about music."

"I don't see the point," she says, following me down the hallway. "You don't need musical training these days to hit it big. Music producers don't even expect you to have a good voice. They just shove everything through Auto-Tune and out pops a hit single. It's more important to develop a good image than to waste your time with lessons and stuff"

"I'm not trying to get a hit single, Meg," I say. "I'm joining choral club because I like to sing, and this is a good way to practice and maybe learn a few things"

She looks at me as if I've just sprouted a third eyeball from my forehead.

"That's the craziest thing I've ever heard," she says. "If you really want to sing, you should just sing on your own. You've got a wicked voice. I bet you wouldn't even need Auto-Tune. I'm telling you, Gerri, you need to think about your image. I say this as your friend: choral club is not going to help your image."

"Meg, I don't care about my image. This has nothing to do with trying to be famous."

"Well, last time I checked, people don't try out for *Big Time* if they aren't interested in being famous."

We arrive outside the doorway to Ms. Kogawa's classroom at the same time as Tyler.

"What do you think Kogawa is going to make us do?" he asks me.

"Who knows? This is all new to me."

"I should have picked school paper," he says before opening the door and walking into the classroom.

"Is *he* in choral club?" asks Meg.

"Yeah," I say. "He's doing it for the extracurricular."

"I wonder if there are any spots open," she says, peering through the doorway at him.

"I don't think they use Auto-Tune in choral club," I tell her. "I have to go. I'll text you later."

Ms. Kogawa passes me some papers as I come into the room. It's more sheet music, but a lot simpler than the music we used in practice.

"The goal over the next few weeks," she says, "is for the two of you to become comfortable with basic sight-reading. I don't expect you to get up to the same level as everyone else in the group, and that's fine because a lot of this will be memorization, but you'll find that a bit of hard work on this end will lead to a better understanding of things down the road."

For a few minutes we run scales and do some vocal exercises. Then we start to work on the music she's given us. We stand next to her at the piano as she plays variations on

"Twinkle, Twinkle, Little Star" and "The Farmer in the Dell." It's dead boring, but I slowly begin to make the connection between the notes on the musical scale and the words I'm singing.

After a little while we stop for the day. Ms. Kogawa writes a website address on the board and hands us more sheet music.

"Copy this address down," she says. "This is an online tuning fork. Use it to find middle C and then practice doing these songs at least ten times before rehearsal on Sunday."

I glance at the songs. I've never heard of them, which will make it more interesting when it comes to singing them blind from sheet music.

"Tyler," says Ms. Kogawa, "I've been having a hard time finding a bass to join us in the club. I was wondering if you have any friends who might be up for it. What about Patrick from the track team? He's got a deep speaking voice. Maybe he'd be interested in trying out singing."

Tyler starts to laugh. "Sorry, Ms. Kogawa, but there's no way Patrick is going to join choral club. Let's just say it's not his scene."

"Well, think about it anyway," she says. "You too, Gerri. If anyone comes to mind that might be interested, let me know. They don't even have to go to our school. They just have to be high school aged. We can push through without a bass, but we'd sound a lot fuller if we could find one."

I walk out of the school with Tyler. "Man," he says. "The guys have been giving me a hard enough time about joining chorus without me trying to recruit them."

"It's fun though, isn't it?" I say.

"Yeah," he says. "I like it all right. I'm not telling them that though. They all think I'm only doing it because I need the extracurricular."

"So why *are* you doing it?" I ask.

He shrugs. "Because I love to sing, I guess."

* * *

Sudden death is the point in every season of *Big Time* when all the semifinalists have to compete against one another in front of the judges. I usually love sudden death—it's one of the most exciting and stressful parts of the show—but this year all I can think is how happy I am that I don't have to go through it. Dealing with the judges is hard enough, but the other competitors can be even worse.

I've never thought about how much of a reality show *Big Time* really is until now. It's not just a talent competition; it's a fight to the finish, based on the idea that only one person is good enough to claw their way to the top. This is never more obvious than during the sudden-death round.

Poppy is a naturally friendly and outgoing person, but she also has an awesome voice, which makes her a target. I'm shocked when cameras catch three singers plotting to sabotage her during group survival. Group survival is the first part of sudden death. Contestants are randomly teamed up and then matched against another group, and they have to "sing to survive." Three of the singers on the team that's been chosen to compete against Poppy's actually talk about putting detergent in her water bottle.

"This is insane!" says my mother, who's watching it with me. "It's like *The Hunger Games*!"

Fortunately, someone has enough of a conscience to report the scheme to the producers, and when they're caught on camera, the three guilty kids are kicked off the show. Poppy isn't filled in until after her group performs and makes it to the next round. When she does hear what happened, she loses her composure for the first time and starts crying. When she tries to go into the bathroom, the camera follows her and won't leave her alone.

"Music competition indeed," says my mother, disgusted. She gets up off the couch and leaves the family room. I consider following her, but I really want to see how Poppy does in the one-on-one round. Of course, she is able to pull herself together and does a great job, easily blowing away her competitor, a short guy with what Tim Canon refers to as a "lounge-singer voice."

Now she's on to the finals. It's good news for Poppy, but for some reason I'm not all that happy for her.

When the show ends, I turn off the TV and go upstairs to my room to practice my sight-reading one more time before the second choral rehearsal tomorrow. I've been practicing every night since Tuesday. At first I just sang from the music that Ms. Kogawa gave Tyler and me, but after a couple of times I knew the melody by heart and it started to feel like cheating, so I printed a bunch of other songs off the Internet and started learning them as well.

I don't need to be very loud when I'm practicing—I just quietly sing along to the sheet music—but I keep my door closed anyway, because I don't really want anyone to watch or hear me. It's really different to be approaching music this way, slowly and carefully, instead of just jumping in the way I always have in the past. I like it though. I like knowing that I'm going to work with other people to build something from the ground up. Right now, I think I prefer that to standing by myself in front of a bunch of judges, waiting for them to decide if I'm any good or not.

Nine

I arrive at rehearsal a bit early the next day. Ms. Kogawa isn't there yet, and Macy and Davis are sitting on the floor outside the locked class-room. I drop my bag and sit down across from them.

"You want some halvah?" asks Davis, handing me a Tupperware container.

"What is it?" I ask, pulling out a piece.

"Hippie fudge," he says.

"It's actually a Middle Eastern dessert," says Macy.

"That hippies feed their kids instead of real fudge," says Davis.

"We're vegan," explains Macy.

"For the time being," says Davis. "Oh man, I am going to eat all the hamburgers when I ungraduate and leave home."

"Ungraduate?" I ask.

"We're unschooled," says Macy. "Most people would call us homeschooled, but that's a different kind of thing. We don't have classes or structured study. We just kind of learn about what interests us."

"And sometimes what interests our parents," says Davis.

"That too," says Macy.

"Wow," I say, after I've had time to pick my jaw up off the floor. "That sounds awesome."

"Most of the time it's pretty cool," says Macy. "As long as we get to do stuff like this."

"Music, you mean?"

"Music and sports and stuff that involves other people. Davis is in an amateur radio club with a bunch of middle-aged men."

"Hey," he says. "It's fun. Don't knock it till you've tried it!"

"Why are you in choral?" Macy asks me. "Have you been doing music for long?"

"Not exactly," I tell them. "I mean, I've been singing my whole life, but I've never done any kind of musical training. I guess the real reason I'm doing it is because I auditioned for *Big Time* and didn't make it, so I thought I'd try to get some experience this way and maybe audition again next year."

"What's *Big Time*?" asks Davis.

"Are you serious?" I ask. They both look at me with blank faces. "It's, like, the biggest show on TV. People sing and then judges critique them and then people at home call in and vote for their favorite and then somebody wins and gets a record deal and a car."

"We don't have a TV," explains Macy.

"No offense," says Davis, "but that sounds awful."

We turn and look as Ms. Kogawa and Bernice come around the corner and walk toward us.

"Wow," says Bernice. "You guys are keeners."

"How did your sight-reading practice go, Gerri?" asks Ms. Kogawa as she unlocks the door.

"I think it went pretty well," I tell her.

Unfortunately, it hasn't gone quite as well as I'd hoped. Ms. Kogawa wants to use today's practice to get through four of the songs in our workbook, but after a couple of attempts at starting from scratch, it becomes obvious that neither Tyler nor I can keep up. We revert to our old method, this time with Macy at the piano, and begin to slowly work through the individual parts until we can finally do a full song all the way through.

It's a lot slower this way, but it works better, and eventually Tyler and I start to catch on. Still, I'm happy when Ms. Kogawa tells us to have a seat. We've been rehearsing for two hours and we've only gotten through half the songs we wanted to. I can't help feeling that it's at least partly because of me, and Bernice doesn't help matters.

"It's too bad everyone can't sight-read," she says. "We'd be able to get through so much more during a rehearsal."

"Yeah, too bad, hey?" says Tyler.

Bernice doesn't pick up on his sarcasm. "It's not your fault, guys," she says. "It's just that you don't have a background in music like the rest of us."

I'm getting a little bit sick of hearing Bernice talk about her background.

"We have a couple of things to consider," says Ms. Kogawa. "We should really start thinking about developing a performance piece. We're not there yet, but I think we will be soon, if we all work hard. It would be great to kick off our year with something of our own ready to go. We should start thinking about where we might want to have our debut performance too."

"What kind of song are we going to do?" asks Olive.

"Ultimately that will be up to you guys," she says. "But I think it would be fun to do a mashup, where we take two songs and bring them together, so start thinking of some possibilities to discuss next week, and we'll work from there."

"How do you know what songs will sound good together?" asks Macy.

"A lot of it is instinct," says Ms. Kogawa. "Some songs just sound great together—they have similar tempos and structure. Mood is important too. I think it would be really neat if we could pick songs with different musical styles, but that's not totally necessary as long as they sound good. We should probably pick something that's got good energy too, since we'll hopefully be doing it for an audience."

"What kind of audience?" I ask.

"I'm not sure yet." She smiles at us. "I'll figure something out. I know I don't want to keep these beautiful voices all to myself. Speaking of beautiful voices, I need everyone to take one last shot at thinking of someone who can possibly step in as a bass for us. It would be great to have the low register covered. Come on, guys, one of you must know somebody who fits the bill."

I'm looking around at the blank faces in the room when I realize I do know somebody. The only problem is, I don't know how to find him.

* * *

Meg is only too eager to help me figure out how to contact Keith.

"You didn't even get his last name?" she asks.

"No," I tell her. "Except for the audition and a couple of minutes at the mall, I've barely even talked to the guy."

We're in my room. Meg is on my laptop, trying to find him online. She does a quick Facebook search and comes up with a bunch of Keiths who go to local high schools. I stand behind her and peer over her shoulder as she scrolls through the list, but I don't recognize any of them.

"This is probably pointless," I say, sitting back down on my bed. "I tried to find him on Facebook too. He's either not on it or he has pretty tight privacy settings."

"Don't be so quick to give up," she says. "We're just getting started. Haven't you seen *CSI*? We just have to dig a little bit deeper."

"I don't even know what to say if we find him," I say.

"I think you're going to have to explain this to me one more time," she says. "Why exactly are you looking for this guy?"

"The choral group needs a bass," I say. "A deep male voice."

"He'll probably be all over that," she says. "Guys love when girls ask them to join nerdy music clubs."

"Maybe you're right," I say. "Maybe he'll think it's stupid."

"Relax," she says. "I'm just joking. Kind of. It's a reason to get in touch with a cute guy, at least."

She closes her eyes and chews on her lip, her fingers hovering over the keyboard. Then she starts typing, quickly throwing different word combinations into the search box.

"Is this him?" she asks after a few seconds. I come back over and look at the screen. Sure enough, it's Keith's face in a YouTube window.

"That's him!" I say.

"He has his own channel," she says, clicking through. Not only does he have his own channel, but he's posted dozens of videos and has a ton of followers. Meg plays one video and we watch as Keith says hey to his audience, then picks up his guitar and begins to play and sing. It's an old blues tune and it sounds really great. His guitar playing is excellent, and his voice is deep and smooth. I know he could easily sing the bass parts for choral. When the song ends, we start another one, then another. He plays lots of blues and folk music, some of his own stuff and even a few newer songs that he's put his own twist on.

"He's good, hey?" I ask.

"Yeah," she says. "Now we just have to leave him a comment and tell him to get in touch with you."

"Do you think that's a good idea? Maybe he'll be embarrassed that I found him this way."

"He has his own online fan base, Gerri. Something tells me he isn't a shy daisy." She scrolls down to the comments section of his most recent video and is about to type something, but I stop her.

"Let me do it," I say. She gets up and I sit at my desk to write a quick message.

Hey, Keith. This is Gerri from the Big Time auditions. I really like your videos, they're great. I was wondering if you could get in touch with me, I have a question to ask you. About music.

"What's with 'about music'?" asks Meg.

"I don't want him to think I'm asking him out or something," I say.

"Yeah, 'cause that would be awful, right? You should take that out. Leave him guessing a bit."

I take that part out, leave an email address and post the comment. To my surprise, he responds within ten minutes.

Hey, Gerri, great to hear from you! Do you want to meet for coffee sometime?

"That sounds promising," says Meg.

"I told you, it's not like that. We need a bass for choral, that's all."

"Suit yourself," she says, "but I wouldn't be so quick to assume the only thing he's interested in is your voice."

Ten

Keith and I meet for coffee after school the next day, at a place downtown called Human Bean. I've never been there before. It's really cool. There's colorful oversized artwork hanging on the exposed brick walls, funky old furniture and a raised stage at the back.

I get there first and order a chai latte, then grab a table in the corner and try to figure out how to bring up choral club with Keith. I haven't mentioned anything to Ms. Kogawa about the possibility of him joining us, because I honestly have no idea what he'll think of it. In the meantime, I need to figure out how to explain it to him.

I don't have much time to think about it, because he shows up shortly after my drink arrives. He's got his guitar slung across his back, and he orders a coffee before scanning the café. I catch his eye, and he waves and heads to the table.

"Hey, Gerri!" he says, carefully placing his coffee on the table before leaning the guitar in the corner.

"You take your guitar everywhere, don't you?" I ask.

"Pretty much," he says. "I do some busking, and I'm in a couple of groups with some people from school. Nothing serious, but we try to practice at school during lunch hour and stuff. Lately I've been trying to hit up open mics with some of those guys."

"Wow," I say. "You're busy."

"Yeah," he says, smiling. "Music's everything. I try to play as much as I can."

I turn to glance at the stage in the corner of the coffee shop. "Is this one of the places where you do open mic?"

"Yeah," he says. "Human Bean is pretty cool, hey? The owners are really great. They love to give local musicians a place to play."

"That's great," I say. I'm beginning to think that Keith's scene is a lot cooler than anything I have to offer. A choral group at another school is probably the last thing he's interested in.

"So what did you want to ask me?" he says.

"Oh, it seems kind of stupid now," I say.

"Try me," he says.

"I'm in a choral club, at my school," I say.

"Cool," he says. "You mean like multiple harmonies, a cappella stuff?"

"Yeah," I say. "I'm a soprano. It's kind of a new thing for me. Anyway, we need a guy who can sing bass, and I know you have a deep voice and all, and I was watching your videos and..."

"I'd love to, if I have time," he says. "That sounds awesome."

"What?" I say. "I haven't even asked you anything yet."

"You're wondering if I'll try out for your choral group, right? I think it sounds cool."

"Are you serious?" I ask him.

"Totally," he says. "I told you, I love music. Any chance I have to try something new, bring it on. I don't have a lot of experience singing with other people, and this sounds like it would be a great way to learn."

I'm so surprised he's up for it that I don't really know what to say. "We practice on Sundays," I say. "We don't even have any performances lined up or anything. Right now we're just doing show tunes and stuff. You might not like it."

He laughs. "Are you trying to convince me not to do it? At least let me give it a shot before you talk me out of it."

"Sorry," I say. "I'm just surprised that you agreed to do it."

"You know," he says, "the group could do a performance here sometime. Open mic means open to anyone who wants to get up and do a song or two."

"Really?" I say. "Don't you think that kind of thing might not, I don't know, fit in?"

"You'd be surprised," he says. "Pretty much any kind of musical act you can imagine plays here for open mic. On one of the nights I played with my friends, there was an old-time banjo player and later an opera singer did an aria. The variety is what makes it fun."

I've never imagined that singing in choral could lead to performances in places like this.

I'd kind of expected we'd be more likely to sing at school assemblies and ribbon-cutting ceremonies.

"You should mention that to Ms. Kogawa," I tell him. "She's the choir director."

"So what made you join choral?" he asks.

"I wasn't planning on it," I tell him. "I was pretty bummed out when I got rejected by *Big Time*, and I was thinking that I'd never try out again, and then Ms. Kogawa asked if I wanted to join. The more I thought about it, the more I realized that I could actually learn something and be better prepared for my audition next year."

"So you think you'll go back and try out again?" he asks.

"Yeah," I say. "I've wanted to be on *Big Time* for years. If I can be better prepared next time, why not? Won't you? Try out again, I mean."

"I doubt it," he says. "I wasn't doing it for the show. Not really. I don't really care about *Big Time*. I just like to try out any new opportunity to play and perform." He shrugs. "It was just one more place to sing."

* * *

I tell Ms. Kogawa about Keith on Tuesday when Tyler and I are in her class for extra help.

"That's wonderful, Gerri!" she says. "I've been a bit worried that we'd have to go the whole year without a bass. You say this guy is musical?"

"Yeah, he plays a few instruments, and he writes his own stuff too. He's going to come to rehearsal on Sunday."

"That's just great," she says. "Speaking of writing, have either of you had a chance to think about our mashup?"

"I haven't had time," says Tyler. "Between school, chorus and track, I'm too busy as it is. Besides, I'm sure the musical wonder will figure something out."

I smile. *Musical wonder—that's good.*

"Who is the musical wonder?" asks Ms. Kogawa.

"Come on," says Tyler. "Bernice. She's way better than us."

"I don't think so at all," she says. "Bernice is very talented, but so are both of you. So is everyone."

Tyler just shrugs. "I guess so."

Ms. Kogawa looks at me. "Have you thought about performance pieces?" she asks.

"Not really," I say. "I don't really understand how it works." That's not entirely true. I've been playing around with different songs in my head since Sunday, and I've actually had a couple of ideas of some tunes that would blend well together. I'm not confident enough to suggest them though. I don't understand music theory, and I'm only barely starting to understand how to read music. I'm pretty sure that any idea I bring up will have something wrong with it. I'm with Tyler—let the musical wonder figure it out.

"Suit yourselves," says Ms. Kogawa, "but I don't think either of you should refrain from bringing ideas to the group. That's half the fun. But it's clear that neither of you are totally comfortable with reading music yet, so maybe when you've progressed a bit you'll be more willing to add your suggestions to the mix."

We spend almost an hour doing more sight-reading, and by the end of the class she seems happy with our progress. I might not be as far along as I'd like to be, but I'm on the way, and it feels good.

Eleven

When I arrive at practice on Sunday, there's no sign of Keith.

"He said he would be here," I tell Ms. Kogawa.

"Don't worry," she says. "We'll get started without him, and if he shows up late we can just fill him in on what's going on."

As Tyler predicted, Bernice has charged full steam ahead on creating a mashup. She passes around neatly stapled pages of lyrics and music, and I notice that she's even written it all out in musical notation and everything.

"Wow," says Ms. Kogawa. "You've really done a lot of work on this."

"I figured if I was going to do it, I should do it properly," says Bernice.

Unfortunately, the songs she's picked aren't my idea of a good time. One of them is "Love Doesn't Die," a drippy ballad that I recognize as the theme to some stupid action movie from a few years ago. I've never heard the other one, "The Brightest Star in Space," but Bernice informs us that it's the biggest hit from a recent Broadway musical called *Love You to the Moon*. She's certainly done a lot of work mashing them together. They're both perfectly arranged and organized so that the focus shifts from one to the other, blending at appropriate moments. There's no denying that they'll fit together well—just humming them in my head tells me that much—but they're very slow and overly dramatic, which makes them kind of similar. I thought the idea was to combine two totally different songs. I'm not about to stick my hand up though. I doubt I could explain what I mean if I tried, and I'm sure Bernice would just remind me I don't have a background in music theory.

"Has anyone else got any ideas?" asks Ms. Kogawa.

"Davis and I kind of played around with a couple of songs," says Macy. "We thought it might be kind of cool to start with something really cutesy, like a nursery rhyme, and then mash it up with something heavy, like a hard-rock song."

"Did you come up with anything specific?" Ms. Kogawa asks.

They glance at each other and then Davis counts back from three and they start to sing. Macy begins by singing "Pop Goes the Weasel" and then Davis comes in with "Rock and Roar," by the heavy-metal band Burn Unit. At first it sounds kind of nuts, but soon they begin to weave together in a unique and surprisingly catchy way. It's funny and impressive at the same time. After a couple of verses they stop, and Davis takes an exaggerated bow.

"That's what I'm talking about!" yells Tyler, as we applaud. Bernice smiles stiffly and claps politely, but I can tell she isn't as impressed as the rest of us.

"Well," says Ms. Kogawa, "that's the kind of creativity I was looking for. From all of you," she hastens to add, smiling at Bernice. "Macy and Davis, do you think you could try to transcribe your piece?"

"Sure," says Davis. "We could probably do that this week."

"Are we really going to sing that one?" asks Bernice. She looks out of sorts. "Don't get me wrong, it's...funny or whatever, but isn't it kind of inappropriate?"

"I don't think so at all," says Ms. Kogawa. "I think it's a lot of fun, and I don't see any reason why we can't try workshopping both of these ideas. Maybe we'll add both to our repertoire. Let's break into groups. Olive, why don't you join Macy and Davis and help them out, and Gerri and Tyler, you guys work with Bernice. It will be a good opportunity to practice some theory. I'm sure Bernice will be able to teach you guys a few things, and you can give her a couple of new perspectives on her mashup."

It's obvious that Bernice has been hoping she would just get to take charge of things herself, but she manages to smile it off. I exchange a look with Tyler, who is obviously as unexcited about this as I am.

There's a knock on the door, and I look over to see Keith's face peering in the window at us. He grins and waves when he sees me. Ms. Kogawa opens the door to let him in.

"You must be Keith," she says.

"Sorry I'm late."

"We haven't started rehearsing yet," she says. "Come on in."

It doesn't take long to realize that Keith will fit right in with the group. Not only is he a bass, but he's got a really strong voice, so he's able to fill in the empty space by himself even though all the other parts have two people singing them. I can see immediately why Ms. Kogawa was so persistent about finding a bass for choral—as we run through our pieces, they just sound fuller and more complete. Keith looks like he's having fun too, which makes me happy, since I'm the one who invited him to try out. I start to wonder if Meg is right, if maybe he is interested in me. Unfortunately, Ms. Kogawa tells him to work with Macy, Davis and Olive on their mashup. I was hoping I'd get a chance to hang out with him a bit more.

One unexpected surprise from the practice is that I'm able to keep up with the songs a lot better. I still have to stop and listen often, but I'm picking up on reading quicker than I thought I would. Even just a few weeks of practice have made a big improvement on what I'm able to do.

"That was really great," says Keith as we're packing up after rehearsal. "I'm glad you told me about this."

"Awesome," I say.

"How do you guys know each other, anyway?" asks Olive.

I'm almost embarrassed to say, but Keith doesn't seem to care. "We met at the *Big Time* auditions," he says.

Olive's eyes widen. "You guys tried out for *Big Time*? That's so cool! What was it like?"

Keith and I look at each other and laugh.

"It wasn't exactly what I expected," I say. "I definitely wish I'd been more prepared."

I'm about to tell Olive that I joined choral club to get more experience for next year's auditions, but Bernice jumps in before I have the chance.

"*Big Time* is such a joke," she says.

"Well, I guess the joke's on us," says Keith, obviously unfazed by Bernice and her background.

"I just mean, all these people with no musical training at all, lining up like sheep just to be insulted," says Bernice.

"Keith has a musical background," I say.

"Yeah, sure," she says. "I'm not talking about you guys, of course. There are always some good performers. It's just amazing how many people think they deserve to be professional musicians without ever having stepped on a stage in their lives."

"I don't mind," says Olive. "And I don't care how mean Tim Canon is, either. I'm gonna be first in line for auditions next year."

"Suit yourself," says Bernice. "Who knows? Maybe you'll win the whole thing."

* * *

I don't know about next year, but it sure seems like this year might be Poppy's. One week after another, I watch as she survives the judges' critiques and the voting public to make it through to the next round. She's a fan favorite—every week there are more people in the studio audience holding signs with pictures of bright red poppies and *FLOWER POWER* written around them in glittery block letters.

The judges are fans too—even Tim Canon is usually able to muster up something nice to say about her performance, and Maria Tillerman, who hasn't seemed particularly cheerful this season, often calls Poppy her breath of fresh air. Poppy is always gracious and appreciative when the fans are going crazy for her or the judges are giving her compliments. I can't help but imagine myself onstage in her place, and I wonder if I'm developing the kind of stage presence and musical confidence that would allow me to take it in stride the way she does.

I also wonder how I'd manage to sing the many different genres of music that *Big Time* features. Most of them would be out of my comfort zone, and although Poppy always manages to stretch her face into that big beautiful smile and deliver the goods, it's hard to believe she's really a big fan of some of the music she has to sing. Hard-rock week is followed by disco classics which leads into country shakedown. I doubt Poppy has spent much time singing that kind of stuff in the past.

I guess performing in a choral group is kind of similar, as we're singing a lot of songs that I wouldn't be otherwise, but it's different in that we work through those songs together, trying to find a common sound. On *Big Time*, the production is slick and prearranged, and Poppy and the other contestants have less than a week to choose, learn and rehearse songs they aren't even familiar with. If I ever do make it onto *Big Time*, I'm pretty sure that that will take a lot of getting used to.

I send Poppy a few messages, but I don't hear back from her. Judging by how hard she's working, it doesn't really surprise me. I just hope she's still having fun.

Twelve

As the weeks with choral club go by, music starts to occupy my mind in a way it never has before. I've always picked up lyrics and melodies easily, and I still find it easy to slide comfortably into a song, to pick out the harmony that needs singing and plug it in like a missing puzzle piece. The big change now, however, is that I have a much better understanding of what's happening when I do it. It's not just instinct anymore—it's backed up by theory.

With every passing Sunday, I feel a bit more confident in my abilities when I show up at rehearsal. Tyler and I have been making good progress with Ms. Kogawa, who's started to teach us a bit of basic theory—harmonics and transposition and other concepts I was never aware of before. Although music is becoming a structured and rehearsed thing for the first time for me, it doesn't make it less fun. In fact, it's just the opposite. I feel more in control, as if practicing and learning the building blocks of music are giving me new insights into what you can do with voices, instruments and a melody.

Ms. Kogawa starts all of my Tuesday sessions with Tyler, as well as the weekly rehearsals, with a vocal warm-up. We run scales, play silly games with our voices and do musical rounds, faster and faster with every turn so that we end up stumbling over words and laughing breathlessly. It's like doing laps and push-ups before soccer practice. The warm-ups stretch our vocal cords so that by the time we get into the actual music, our voices are limber and ready to roll.

*   *   *

My family goes to visit Granddad for his birthday. We hang out in the lounge with his friends and watch him open presents. Seeing Granddad surrounded by the many nice people he's gotten to know at Lilac Grove, I'm reminded of his sad early days here, and I'm grateful once again for his guitar. The staff in the kitchen have baked him a special cake, and after we've watched him blow out the candles and everyone's had a piece, Dina leans forward in her chair.

"I can't think of a better reason to break out a few songs, Nelson," she says.

"No argument here," he says.

Jack runs to Granddad's room to get his guitar, and when he comes back we all pull our chairs into a circle and spend the next hour or so enjoying a good old-fashioned sing-along. We run through some of the old songs I've heard Granddad play for as long as I can remember, and then other residents of the home begin shouting out requests. A lot of them aren't his style, but Granddad seems to know them all, from jazz standards to wartime big band anthems to sixties folk songs. Nobody knows all the words to the songs, but it doesn't matter—there are enough people who know various bits and pieces that the rest of us pick up what we can and the music keeps rolling along.

I watch Granddad play one tune after another, amazed that he has so many chords and lyrics and melodies stored in his mind. At one point or another, he took the time to memorize each one of these songs, and now he's able to access them, belt them out, share them with the world. Keith has the same kind of dedication and wants to learn as much as he can about music. It's not just a skill or a hobby, it's a passion. I'm starting to feel that way too.

"How about it, Gerri?" asks Granddad. I snap out of my daydream and realize that the music has stopped and everyone's looking at me.

"Sorry, what did you ask?"

"How's about doing a duet with your old granddad?" he asks. "One from the old days."

"I thought these were all from the old days," says Jack, and everyone laughs.

"Sure, Granddad," I say. "What were you thinking?"

He starts playing and I recognize the song right away, and when he finishes the intro, I'm prepared to sing along with him.

Oh, Shenandoah, I long to see you,
Away, you rolling river
Oh, Shenandoah, I long to see you,

Away, I'm bound away
'Cross the wide Missouri...

I expect people to pick up the words and begin to sing along as we get further into it, but everyone stays silent, letting the two of us sing this one together. I get so caught up in the music that I forget there's anyone listening to us until the song ends and they break into loud applause. I glance over at my parents and am surprised to see them beaming—my dad's eyes have even welled up with tears.

It's not like there are all that many people here, but it's obvious that we've made an impact. I can't imagine feeling any better if I'd just performed for a live studio audience.

"I can't remember you ever sounding even half as good as you did today, Gerri," my mother says as we're driving home.

"It was beautiful," says Dad.

"I'm just going to come out and say it," says Mom. "I'm happy you didn't get picked by *Big Time*. This choral group is the best thing that's ever happened to you."

"Thanks," I say. "I'm learning a lot. I think I'll be a lot more prepared for next year's auditions."

"Tyler says you guys have a show lined up," says Jack. "What's that all about?"

Mom turns around, her eyes wide. "What?! Where? When?"

"It's not really a show," I tell them. "We're going to perform a couple of songs at an open mic downtown. It's not a big deal."

"You bet it's a big deal," says Dad. "As if you weren't going to tell your parents about your first public performance!"

The truth is, I haven't been looking forward to the Human Bean open mic. When Keith mentioned it to Ms. Kogawa, she jumped all over it, calling the managers and making sure it would be okay for us to do two numbers. Now we're booked in for the end of the month, which only gives us a few weeks to practice.

That would all be fine except for the fact that working with Bernice on her mashup has been zero fun. She's determined to keep the piece pretty much exactly the way she imagined and wrote it in the first place, which means it's as lame now as it was the day she proposed it, even though we've been meeting for an hour a week to work on it. At least, Bernice and I have been meeting for an hour a week. After a couple of meetings Tyler stopped showing up, blaming it on college applications and track practice.

It's not like I can blame him, but I don't have good excuses like he does, so I'm stuck with her. I'm intimidated enough by her background that I have a hard time making suggestions, and on the few occasions I try, she shoots them down. Eventually, I give up altogether and spend the weekly meeting sitting on the couch in her basement, watching her play the parts again and again on her piano.

Ms. Kogawa has started breaking up Sunday rehearsal into two segments. During the first half, we work on Macy and Davis's mashup, which is super fun to sing and is getting better with every week, thanks to Olive's and Keith's contributions. In the second half of rehearsal, we do Bernice's, which practically puts us all to sleep.

A couple of weeks out from our performance, Ms. Kogawa tells us that we need to lock things down.

"Take some time this week to iron out the final bugs in your pieces," she says. "Next week we'll do a last rehearsal before the open mic. I've decided that we'll start with Bernice's piece. It's slower, so it will get the crowd used to us and give us a chance to showcase our vocals. Then we'll finish with the faster piece, because it will pump the crowd up."

"I think she means wake them up," Tyler whispers to me.

We run through each of the songs from start to finish before wrapping up for the day. Bernice heads toward me as I'm filling my backpack. Tyler glances over and bolts when he sees her coming.

"I was thinking we should get together one more time tomorrow and make sure everything's in order with the piece," Bernice says. "Can you come to my house after supper?"

"I can probably do that," I say.

"I guess there's no point asking Tyler," she says. "Even when he does show up, he doesn't contribute anything."

I'm left wondering what it is she thinks I contribute, but I'm not about to make an issue out of it.

Keith comes up to me as I'm leaving. "Hey, Gerri," he says. "You interested in grabbing a coffee at Human Bean?"

My heart skips a beat. *Is this a date?*

"Sure," I say. "Sounds great."

"Cool," he says. "Macy and Davis and I were just gonna hang out for a while and talk about the mashups."

It's a bit of a letdown that he isn't actually asking me out, but I'm still happy to tag along with them. I've been wishing I was in their group since the day Ms. Kogawa assigned us. One of the things I've regretted most about the way she broke up the class is that while working with Bernice is a boring chore, the other group has gotten really friendly. I know that they've been hanging out regularly and messing around with other ideas for songs, which sounds like a lot more fun than sitting in Bernice's basement twiddling my thumbs.

Macy has their parents' car, so she drives us downtown to the café. Inside, we grab seats near the empty stage. I hadn't noticed how small it is before.

"We'll be crowded up there, hey?" I say.

"Yeah," says Keith. "We'll probably have to spill over onto the floor."

"Maybe we can arrange it so that Bernice ends up standing in the bathroom and we can conveniently forget to do her song," says Davis.

Macy elbows him in the arm.

"Sorry, Gerri," he says. "I forgot you were here. Your group's song is lovely and emotional."

I laugh. "You don't have to worry about offending me," I say. "I don't really have anything to do with it. I just show up and she tells me what to do."

"You shouldn't let her get away with that," says Macy.

"It's true," says Keith. "You're really good. You could bring a lot to the song if she'd let you."

I'm surprised to hear them talk like this, as if I have something to contribute besides my voice.

"I don't really know much about that stuff," I say.

"What stuff? Music stuff?" asks Keith. "Come on, Gerri. You've got a great voice, and you have a better ear for harmony than anyone else in the group."

"I don't know what you're talking about," I say. "I don't even know how to read music that well."

"You're learning though," says Macy. "You really have a great sense of what sounds good. It's not just being able to sing a melody line—it's being able to interpret it, to know when to sing loud or soft, how to balance with other singers. It's really cool. Anyone can learn to read music and understand theory. The hard part is the stuff that comes naturally to you."

My first impulse is to assume they're just being nice, but they look totally serious. What if they're right? What if I'm actually talented, not just with a decent voice but with a good head for music? Not that it really matters now, at least as far as the song is concerned. Our last meeting is tomorrow, and it's not like I can come up with any suggestions by then, let alone convince Bernice to take them.

"The problem," says Davis, echoing my thoughts, "is that it really doesn't make much difference at this point."

"Doesn't hurt to try," says Keith.

"I wouldn't know how to begin," I say.

"How did you guys figure out your songs?" Keith asks Macy and Davis.

"We just kind of messed around with different songs and stuff," says Macy.

"Only took an hour or so to get the basic idea down," says Davis. "The rest was just figuring out how to make it work."

"I don't think I can come up with anything that quick," I say.

"Don't worry about it," says Macy. "I'm sure it will all sound great when we have the chance to do it in front of an audience."

None of them look all that convinced, though.

Thirteen

fter we leave Human Bean and Macy drops me off at home, I can't get their suggestion out of my mind. I keep running through "Love Doesn't Die" and "The Brightest Star in Space" in my head, trying to drop a new song into the center, something that will make the other two sound different the way "Pop Goes the Weasel" turns "Rock and Roar" into something unique.

Eventually, I just give up. It's too hard to imagine introducing something to those two dramatic, powerful songs that will help make a new sound. By the time Dad calls me down to eat, I've pretty much decided that Keith, Macy and Davis were mistaken about my abilities.

"Go call your mother in from the garden, will you, Gerri?" Dad asks as he dishes up spaghetti.

I yell into the shadows at the back of the yard and grab a seat at the table. Mom comes in a few moments later, her hair a mess and her hands covered with dirt. She looks totally frustrated.

"What happened to you?" Dad asks as she washes up.

"Oh, it's that stupid lilac stump near the shed," she says. "I spent almost two hours hacking at it with an ax, digging as far down around the roots as I could, and it won't come out."

"Why don't you just leave it in the ground?" asks Jack.

"I can't leave it there," she says, "because I want to plant a new perennial bed on that spot, and the stump is in the way. Nothing will be able to put down roots because there's a big hunk of dead wood taking up all the space."

"That's it!" I exclaim. Everyone turns to look at me.

"What's it, sweetheart?" asks Dad.

"Sorry," I say. "I just got an answer for a homework question."

I hurry through supper, then race up to my room and go online. The problem with the two songs Bernice chose, I've realized, is that they're just too powerful together. For something else to fit in and change the sound, one of them has to be removed completely. I doubt Bernice will agree to it, but at least nobody can say I didn't try, even if no one ever hears what I come up with. I almost want to do this more for my own satisfaction than to change Bernice's composition.

I spend more than an hour watching videos and listening to songs online, closing my eyes and trying as hard as I can to imagine how each song could drop into "Love Doesn't Die," but nothing seems to work.

After I've unsuccessfully run through what seems like a hundred options, I groan and spin around in my chair, wondering if there's any point at all. That's when I glance across my room, and everything clicks into place.

*   *   *

I walk to Bernice's house early the next evening, wondering how I'm going to bring up my idea. It turns out to be easier than I expected.

She opens the door before I even have a chance to knock.

"Come on in," she says. "We need to get to work." She waits impatiently as I take off my shoes, then bounds down the stairs to the rec room so fast that I can barely keep up. She drops onto her piano stool and looks at me frantically.

"What's the matter, Bernice?" I ask. She's acting bizarre.

"It just isn't working!" she says.

"What do you mean?"

"My—I mean our—mashup," she says. "I tried to do everything properly. I picked songs that have similar tempos and are in the same time signature, but it just doesn't work!" She pauses and looks at me almost desperately. "You need to help me out—you've got a good ear. You need to help me make the harmonies more exciting or something."

I'm so astonished at how stressed out she sounds that I barely register her compliment.

"Bernice, it isn't that bad," I say.

"Oh give me a break," she says. "I know everyone hates it."

"Bernice," I say. "You're being too hard on yourself. Your mashup is great, technically. It's just that—"

"What?!" she asks, spinning around on her piano stool and leaning toward me.

"Well," I say, "you could stand to loosen up a bit, let things come a bit more naturally."

Her face pinches up and I expect her to snap at me, but instead she spins back around and drops her head onto the keyboard, filling the basement with a mournful, discordant drone. "I don't know, maybe you're right," she says, her face smooshed into the keys. "It's too late though. There's no time to do anything different. There's only one rehearsal between now and the show. We don't have time to figure anything out."

"Maybe you're wrong about that," I say.

She raises her head and looks at me. "What do you mean?"

"Well, I might have a solution," I tell her. "But I think we should get Tyler over to help. He's supposed to be part of our group, and I think he can contribute something."

Tyler and I text back and forth for a few minutes. He's understandably hesitant, but once I explain what's going on, he agrees to come over and try to help.

At first Bernice doesn't understand what I'm trying to do, but Tyler picks it up quickly, and once we start singing out the different pieces, she begins to come on board. It turns out that we're a pretty good team. I have the tune in my head, but it's not much more than a rough concept when we start. Once Bernice understands the idea, she applies some theory to it, and slowly it all starts to come together. Tyler is able to do the tenor parts and has several good ideas about how the two songs could relate to each other lyrically. By the time Mom comes to pick me up, near midnight, all three of us are feeling pretty good about what we've accomplished.

Ms. Kogawa is a harder sell. We stop at the music room to see her before classes begin the next morning, and at first she doesn't like the idea of changing things this close to the performance at all.

"Guys," she tells us, "the piece is going to go over very well."

"Sorry, Ms. Kogawa, but I don't think that's true," says Tyler. "It's a total snoozefest."

"That's not very nice, Tyler," she says. "Bernice put a lot of work into that piece, and it's very technically accomplished."

"No, he's right," says Bernice. "It's super boring."

"Even if I agreed with that, which I don't," she says, "we have four other people to think about here. We've been working on this piece for weeks. How do you expect people to take it when we tell them we want to go back to the drawing board after they've already put all this work in?"

"I wouldn't worry about that," I tell her. "I'm pretty sure everyone else is willing to change things if it makes for a better show."

"At least let us try to sing it for you," says Bernice.

Ms. Kogawa sighs and looks at her watch. "Okay," she says. "You'll have to be quick though— the bell is going to ring in a few minutes."

We're prepared for this and quickly break into the piece, stopping just before the bell starts to ring. Ms. Kogawa waits for it to stop and then looks at us for a long moment.

"You're right," she says. "It's much better. We'll bring it to the group and see what they say. If they're willing to put in the extra time, we can switch it."

Fourteen

Considering the conversation I had with Keith and Macy and Davis, it's no surprise that everyone's on board to change songs for the open mic. When Bernice and Tyler and I unveil the changes at the beginning of rehearsal on Sunday, I can practically hear a sigh of relief ripple through the room.

"It's going to take a lot of hard work to get things ready for Saturday," Ms. Kogawa says. Nobody argues.

The next six days are among the most fun, stressful and rewarding that I've ever experienced. All seven of us spend hours in Bernice's basement, learning our new parts and fine-tuning the performance as much as we're able to in the limited time we have. Bernice is still pretty bossy, but now that the rest of the group is involved, she's less inclined to walk all over our suggestions. I'm just happy to hear some of my ideas come to life. It feels great.

"Fun, hey?" Keith asks me at one point when we've taken a short break from practicing to eat a snack that Bernice's mother has brought downstairs for us.

"Totally," I say.

"This is why I try to get involved in as much music as I can," he says. "When you're learning a new tune or practicing for a new kind of gig, it always starts off messy and noisy and confusing, but if you give yourself the chance to work out the kinks and discover the sound, there's no better feeling."

I know what he means. A couple of months ago, I didn't really know any of these people very well, and now I'm making music with them. It has been messy, and definitely confusing, but I can't remember the last time I felt this satisfied about anything.

"Maybe you want to hang out sometime," he says. "To mess around with some songwriting and stuff."

"That sounds fun," I say.

"I mean the two of us," he says. "Like, hanging out, or whatever."

He starts to blush, and finally I catch on to what he's saying.

"For sure," I manage to say, trying not to sound flustered. "That would be really cool."

"Awesome," he says. We grin goofily at each other, not sure what to say, before he spins on his heel and goes over to the coffee table to grab a cookie.

* * *

On the day of the show, we meet up at the school and head to Human Bean together.

The audience is a lot bigger than I'd expected. Keith has mentioned that there's usually a good crowd on open-mic nights, but he didn't say that it's standing room only. By the time we arrive, my family, including Granddad, has staked a claim at a table in the corner with a good view of the stage. Meg is sitting with them, and she waves wildly when she spots me.

"You didn't mention how cute the baristas are," she says when I go over to say hello to everyone.

"This choral thing sounds better and better by the day!"

"I'm glad you could make it, Granddad," I say, leaning over to give him a hug.

"Are you kidding me?" he says. "As if I'd miss your big debut!"

"I'm going to stand with the rest of the group to watch the show," I tell them.

"Break a leg!" says Dad.

I push through the crowd and squeeze up next to Davis.

"We're on sixth," he tells me. "Keith just went up to check out the list."

A man comes onto the stage and thanks us all for coming out. "I haven't seen this place this packed in years," he says. "I guess that's what happens when six newbies sign up! Everyone they know comes out to cheer them on! Make sure to tip the staff and enjoy the show!"

The acts that come on before us are as diverse as Keith told me they would be. One lady does a decent standup comedy act, and she's followed by a beat boxer who spits and scrapes his way through a Michael Jackson song. A husband and wife get up and sing a couple of really nice songs that they wrote themselves, and when they get off the stage, I'm surprised to see Keith get up with a couple of guys I don't recognize. They bang their way through some high-energy rock music that gets the crowd dancing and cheering. He wasn't kidding about keeping his musical options open. Between this, our choral group and the laid-back surfer music he sang at the *Big Time* audition, he's all over the map.

Our group gives them an extra-loud cheer when they finish, and Keith pushes back toward us, flushed and happy.

"That was awesome!" I tell him.

"Thanks," he says. "Felt good to burn off some energy. Now we just have to wait for the main event!"

After one more act, a girl with a keyboard doing covers of Tori Amos songs, it's our turn.

"Remember to relax and have fun," says Ms. Kogawa as we make our way to the stage. It takes a few moments for us to arrange ourselves properly. Keith, Tyler and Bernice are the tallest, so they stand on the floor in front of the stage and the rest of us stand behind them. I look out at the crowd, catching the excited eyes of my family and Meg in the back corner and noticing the attentive faces of the rest of the crowd. It's not a giant auditorium full of TV cameras like on *Big Time*, but at this moment it's just as exciting. Not to mention nerve-racking.

Ms. Kogawa pulls her tuning whistle out of her pocket and blows a tight clear C note to orient us to the right key, and then we begin.

With serious faces, Bernice and Tyler begin singing, just the two of them at first.

> *Every single day another part of me ages*
> *I keep on flipping through the pages of my life*

Then the rest of us come in, singing the parts Bernice wrote for us. She might be a control freak, but Bernice has a lot of talent, and her transcription is top notch. Boring or not, our voices come together beautifully.

> *The Earth continues turning, the candle keeps*
> *   on burning*
> *But my love, my love never dies*
> *It never dies*
> *It lives forever...*

At this point, the song gradually shifts to something more upbeat and cheerful as we begin to mix in the lyrics of my favorite Marla Belle Munro song.

Forever and ever and ever and ever...

Then I come in.

*You've got that look on your face that says
    never means never,
That our love will last forever, that there's
    nothing that could sever what we've got...*

The audience claps when they hear the dramatic shift in the music, and I hear my granddad holler out from the back of the room. At this point, the rest of the group joins in—Keith singing a deep repetitive bass line, everyone else filling in the lyrics.

*I'd rather die than say goodbye, and when we
    look up at the sky
I think that you and I could fly,
All we'd have to do is try
Come on, baby, let's try...*

From here on, the two songs begin to intertwine, Bernice leading the way on her song and me leading the way on mine, with everyone else singing with and against and around us. By the time we're done the first mashup, the audience is clapping along and enjoying themselves, and we finish to a loud round of applause. There's no time to relax though, and we break immediately into Macy and Davis's mashup. The audience loves this one, and we're having fun too, letting loose and hitting all our notes perfectly. By the time we're done, the room is totally into us, and I feel an electric thrill coming back at us from the crowd.

"That was awesome!" Bernice says to me as we leave the stage. "Thank you so much for helping save the song!"

"I think we all saved the song," I say. "And you're right, that was awesome!"

"Great job, guys!" Ms. Kogawa says when we're all off the stage. "I can't wait to start planning our next show!"

I manage to reach through the crowd and grab Keith's arm to get his attention.

"That was fun, hey?" he asks.

"Totally," I say. "I was thinking about what you were saying the other day. About getting together or whatever. Do you want to do that soon?"

He smiles widely at me. "How about tomorrow?" he asks.

"Perfect."

Still smiling, I squeeze my way over to my family.

"Gerri, you were incredible!" my mother says, reaching up to grab my hands.

"I have to admit," says Meg, "that was way better than I expected."

"Jeez, thanks," I say.

"Hey, it's a compliment!" she says.

"I'm proud of you, Gerri," says Granddad. "You were just as great as I expected."

I hang out with my family, still buzzing from the excitement of being onstage, watching while a harmonica player busts out a couple of blues songs. When he leaves the stage, the announcer comes to the mic.

"Next up," he says, "we've got the old-school country stylin's of Nelson Jones!"

"What's going on, Granddad?" asks Jack.

"You don't think I'm going to let a perfectly good opportunity to play for an audience go to waste, do you?" asks Granddad. He turns and winks at me, then gets up and retrieves his guitar from behind the counter. The audience claps as he climbs cheerfully onto the stage, and the loudest applause in the room comes straight from our table.

Fifteen

Poppy gets cut from *Big Time* a couple of weeks before the finale.

I'm surprised and not surprised all at the same time. On one hand, I still think she had the best voice of anyone on the show. On the other hand, it had become clearer every week that she didn't really fit in to what the producers and the judges wanted. She kept trying to be herself, singing the songs she liked, dressing the way she wanted to, and they kept trying to turn her into something different—slicker and more commercial, a brand-new Poppy.

By the time she was voted off, it was obvious that she wasn't enjoying it as much as she had when she started. Still, I write to tell her how bad

I feel for her, which is the case until I meet her for coffee at Human Bean when she's back in town.

"What a relief, Gerri," she says. "You have no idea!"

"Really?" I ask. "I figured getting voted off would have been super crappy."

"Sure, it was," she says. "But only because I let myself get into that mindset. I stopped caring about the songs I was singing and started obsessing about making it further in the show. I hated the whole *beating people* part of things, and that became more and more what it was about. It was all stress, all the time."

"I can see that," I say.

"Don't get me wrong," she says. "It was a cool experience for a while, having people dress me up and getting to stand on that glitzy stage every week. It was just the way I'd always imagined it. But it stopped being fun after a while. I grew up singing in church and with my family and at school concerts. I sing because I love singing. Not because I wanted to prove I was better than all those other people."

"It's too bad nobody stood up for you," I say.

"Maria Tillerman did," says Poppy. "She tried to, anyway, but the producers weren't really looking for her to make suggestions. They just wanted her to sit in her seat and do her job, same as us, I guess. She's leaving the show anyway."

"What?" I say. "Really?"

"Yeah. She hates it, so she didn't sign a contract for next year. They're waiting until the season ends to make the announcement. I shouldn't even be telling you. After I got kicked off the show, she told me that she's looking forward to making real music for a change. I know the feeling."

Even before talking to Poppy, I'd decided not to try out for *Big Time* again next year. I've got enough on my plate with the choral group. We've started working on a new round of mashups, and Bernice and I are actually working together for real this time, looking for a new way to combine the show tunes she loves with the classic country I'm into.

Keith and I have been hanging out a lot. Sometimes we meet up with Macy and Davis and mess around with different compositions. Sometimes it's just the two of us, and we try to come up with lyrics as he fools around with melodies on his guitar. It's not all music though. We've been to a couple of movies and gone for walks together, and of course we spend a lot of time at Human Bean. Like Meg said, *Big Time* wasn't such a waste of time after all. If I hadn't tried out, I never would have met him.

In fact, it turns out that getting rejected from *Big Time* was one of the best things that could have happened to me. Not just because of Keith, but because it helped me understand what being a musician is really all about. It isn't about getting picked out of a crowd and being told you're the best; it's about learning and practicing and making music wherever and whenever you feel like it.

* * *

It's a beautiful crisp day in early December when I get on the bus to visit Granddad. I'm weighed down a bit, and climbing up the steps is kind of cumbersome, but people smile at me as I walk down the aisle and squeeze myself into a seat.

It's too cold for Granddad to be out on the porch, and I find him in his room. He's in his chair by the window, playing his guitar so intently that he doesn't notice me standing in the doorway.

"Knock knock!" I say. He turns from the window and smiles broadly as I walk over to him and bend down to give him a kiss on the cheek.

"What have you got there, girl?" he asks, pointing at the case hanging across my back.

I unsling the guitar from my shoulder and unzip it from its case. It's not mine—it's one of Keith's. He's letting me borrow it until I decide whether I should really push for one of my own for Christmas.

"I was thinking it might be kind of fun if you taught me a few things, Granddad," I say.

"Make music with my granddaughter?" he says. "I can't think of any way I'd rather spend my time."

I know exactly what he means.

Acknowledgments

As always, thanks to my friends and family for their continued love, support and encouragement. Thanks to everyone at Orca for being such a pleasure to work with. Thank you to Sarah Harvey for creating the awesome Limelights series and for reminding me to always keep the reader at front of mind. Most of all, thank you to Andrew for keeping the train on the tracks and for always believing in me.

TOM RYAN was born and raised in Inverness on Cape Breton Island. He once sat in line overnight to audition for a televised singing competition, only to be told that he was potentially the most boring performer in the world. Ouch. He lives in Ottawa, Ontario, with his partner and dog. *Big Time* is his fourth book. You can find him online at www.tomwrotethat.com.